Willigis: The Old Sage of Atlantis

WILLIGIS

THE OLD SAGE OF ATLANTIS

Bluestar
Communications
Woodside, California

Translated by Ingrid Racz

First published in German under the title:
Der Alte aus Atlantis
by Aquamarin Verlag, Grafing, Germany, 5th Edition, 1993

This translation:
© 1995 Bluestar Communications Corporation
44 Bear Glenn
Woodside, CA 94062
Tel: 800-6-Bluestar

First printing 1995

ISBN: 1-885394-01-2

All rights reserved. No part of this book may be reproduced in any form without the written permission of the publishers, except for brief quotations embodied in critical articles and reviews.

Printed in China

THE OLD SAGE OF ATLANTIS

The ship was laboring sluggishly through a churning Caribbean Sea, with its mountainous waves stacking up in the racing, sweeping storm. The decks were empty, almost all passengers had withdrawn to their cabins, and only the few men still able to hold their drinks sat in the card room, trying to overcome their uneasiness with continued consumption of alcohol.

Having returned to his quarters, Erik von Lichtenau was lying on his couch, abandoned to his thoughts. In his intelligent face, his large eyes were staring into the empty space before him—their gaze turned inward. Von Lichtenau was a descendant of an old aristocratic German family which had held its ancestral seat in southern Germany for centuries. His father had held an office in the court of one of the minor princes of the German Federation but his employment was terminated when the First World War was lost to the Allies and the Empire had collapsed in ruins. The old courtier was unable to come to terms with this blow and had died just a few years later.

Erik von Lichtenau had also lost his dearly beloved mother. She had been everything to him. While her outward appearance was that of an aristocratic lady, moving through life without reproach and fulfilling the numerous social obligations pertaining to her husband's position with both enthusiasm and charm, in her innermost heart she had always been attracted to the mystical and the spiritual. Whenever she could to arrange it, she spent her free time with her books, where her special interest lay in the life and culture of ancient peoples whose history had only in part come to light thus far. Along with the many scholars and scientists who spoke to her through their written works, she attempted to penetrate mysteries which had been hidden under a blanket of impenetrable darkness for thousands of years. Time and again her imagination was fired by the many puzzling mysteries she unearthed, mysteries she would discuss enthusiastically with her son.

An image of his beloved mother appeared in Erik's mind, where he saw her in the circular room atop the tower of their fortress-like castle. It was from this cozy room, a room that had served as their library, that one could see for miles in every direction.

On many occasions, when the twilight hours called upon the shadows of the night to sink down toward the earth, his mother had sat in the big armchair and, with her gaze reaching into the far distance, she had begun to speak, conjuring images of the empires of the Mayas, the Incas and the Etruscans for the precocious boy—images that kindled his curiosity. Those relaxed, informative hours were to become for the boy—and subsequently for the young man—a source of all-embracing insight, as the knowledge flowed to him from his mother's kindly soul.

In her unquenchable thirst for knowledge, for many years his mother had also been captivated by the sunken continent of Atlantis. She had acquired all the relevant books and it was on this journey that Erik had been her close companion, the friend with whom she shared her innermost thoughts on the subject. This is how the same eagerness for knowledge that was hers, an eagerness that had been awakened and nourished in early life, was awakened in her son as well. When she had departed from him, he had begun to apply himself to those fields of knowledge with even more intensity. Over time, there arose in him an ever-growing desire to investigate these things in person, and destiny rose to meet his aspirations by smoothing the path for him. Some years previously, a relative of his mother, one who had been born into a family of Dutch ship owners, had died and appointed her as his heir. Thus, by way of inheritance, her son had been given the very means he needed.

Now nothing could hold him in his homeland or from the company of his books. He had to find out for himself whether there was any truth at all in the many stories he had read. He had been traveling for several years now, starting out from Bremen, traveling first to England, and from there to South America where he had inspected the Inca ruins. Though he had studied every line inscribed on the walls of the partially demolished temples, so far he had been unable to add any new insight to the claims made by the many scholars who had preceded him. The ruins of the Incas revealed nothing new to him, so he had moved on and was now hoping to solve the many puzzles that kept his imagination racing by following the traces of the ancient Mayan civilization in Mexico.

The rolling of the ship seemed to be abating. Lichtenau reached for the notebook lying beside him and started to thumb through it, as though trying to remember something, and then he began to read in a low voice:

"...Mayan: most important city of the ancient Mayan empire. Ruins located about 16 miles south of Merida in Yucatan. Well preserved city wall 18 meters high and 30 meters wide at the level of the foundations. Despite the reconstruction of the entire alphabet, the interpretation of the hieroglyphs and of the inscriptions on the remaining stone monuments has only been partially successful. Only the hieroglyphs representing the months of the year have been deciphered so far...."

Lichtenau stopped reading and was immersed in his reflections once more. "Strange," he thought, "the symbols of the ancient Etruscans—the Raseneans, as they called themselves—also proved impossible to decipher. They too were a people of unknown origin that had suddenly stepped into the light of history with a highly evolved culture. Might it be possible that there was a connection between the Etruscans and the Mayas? If only that mystery could be solved!"

A dreamy meditational mood took hold of Lichtenau, the notebook slipped from his fingers—and images rose up before him.... There were lofty Temples of the Sun..., cyclopean walls surrounding palaces of peculiar architectural style.... But soon these visions began to fade again, to disappear as vapor.

Lunch was announced unexpectedly by the heavy sound of the ship's gong and Lichtenau was drawn from his thoughts. He got up, rearranged his clothes somewhat, left his cabin and went into the dining-hall. He was immediately surrounded by the lively din of voices, as almost all the passengers had taken their seats. Lichtenau was one of the last to arrive. He approached his table, politely—but quickly—bowed to his neighbors and sat down without paying them further attention, as he lost himself immediately in the pleasures of the palate. Somewhat abruptly, a young girl of considerable Latin beauty sitting opposite him, said,

"Why is the Señor so quiet?"

He looked up at her, smiled, and—pointing to his food—he replied,

"Pardon me, Señorita, but I think it's best to give the stomach its due, first."

"Oh—but this is not the way a Caballero should speak!" was her challenging retort.

"Quite possibly, Señorita, but I have no ambition in that direction," said Lichtenau, and he turned back to his plate. Still, he continued to observe the young girl through half-closed eyelids. One had to admit that with those two dark eyes looking cheerfully out into the world from her tawny, oval face Señorita Juanita y Serestro was certainly a beauty. With hair parted down the middle and tied in a knot at the back, hair so black that as it framed her face it almost seemed blue, she was not unlike a southern-style image of the Holy Virgin.

Much to the distress of her chaperone, herself an elderly and somewhat jaded woman, the Señorita had shown interest in the young scholar, in the free and easy manner so typical of her, from the very first moment she had seen him. It was obvious that she got a real thrill out of provoking Lichtenau, pulling him out of his quiet reserve again and again, and, given her chatty ways, he was already rather well informed about her background as well.

Her father was the very wealthy owner of a silver mine in Mexico who always gave her what she wanted. This time he had allowed her to travel to Rio de Janeiro to have a look at that great South American metropolis. Of course, Juanita had a many admirers but she did not take them seriously; she laughed at them and played all manner of wanton tricks on them, often putting her victims in embarrassing situations. Lichtenau was the first man she had not succeeded in hitching to her triumphal chariot—at least not yet!

Although he was always polite and reserved, Lichtenau treated her like a naughty child. Sometimes this treatment made her absolutely furious and when she was in such a mood and happened to speak about him to her traveling companion she would refer to him as "that German dunce." Her chaperone, in turn, was inspired by such words to treat Lichtenau with haughty arrogance.

Señorita Juanita had made up her mind to treat him this way as well but every time she saw Lichtenau and he began conversing with her in his quiet, friendly fashion, she was disarmed. He was so different from all the other younger and older men who courted her. He didn't pay her compliments nor did he seem to notice any change in her attire; he simply treated her with an even friendliness and only at times was there even a smile to break the habitual expression of deep thought on his slender face. A few times he had also spoken to her about his own interests. At first this had bored her but then she began to listen to him with growing interest and her mind became confused over him, causing her much unrest. Her female pride—born from her beauty and wealth—would often rebel against his reserve. On the other hand, she was drawn to his calm, self-assured manner, his pleasant voice and, when he rested his clear gaze upon her, a very peculiar feeling—a sensation she had never experienced with any man before—engulfed her.

"Are you still planning to visit those old ruins of yours?" Juanita asked him.

"Yes, I told you so already, Señorita," was his short answer.

"Why don't you come to Mexico City with us instead? It's a very interesting city and much nicer than your antiquated stones. Papa would certainly be happy to welcome you to our house."

"Perhaps later. It would certainly be an honor to make the acquaintance of your father."

Juanita puffed nervously on her cigarette. "He is like an icebox," she thought. "I wonder, why I am even talking to him at all." Then, suddenly, an idea struck her.

"Where exactly do you want to go, Señor?"

"To the ruins of Mayapan in Yucatan; they are located in the proximity of the village of Telchaquillo, which is not far from Merida," Lichtenau replied.

"Telchaquillo?" the Señorita mused. Then she turned excitedly to her companion: "Telchaquillo—doesn't Papa own some land there too, Dolores? I believe he once said so."

"I don't know anything about that, Señorita. Besides, it is hardly to be expected that Señor y Serestro would allow you to travel to that totally desolate land," Señora Dolores said reprovingly.

"I'm sure I know better than that!" Juanita cried. "Papa will surely let me go there if I want to." And turning toward Lichtenau, she added, "What would you say if I came with you?"

Lichtenau had a sudden urge to laugh out loud.

"Impossible, Señorita! That's no place for a spoiled young lady like you to visit."

Juanita bit her lower lip. A sudden blush moved across her spirited face.

"You are a very horrible man!" she burst out—and then for emphasis she added, "Yes you are!"

"But Señorita...!" Señora Dolores cut in.

"Come on!" Juanita started up in anger. "I'm not a little girl anymore and I know what I want. If Herr von Lichtenau does not take me with him, I shall ask Papa to accompany me to Mayapan and show me those ruins!" She was looking very upset with her eyes flashing and her hands waving nervously.

Lichtenau thought it wise to put an end to their conversation. He stood up, bowed to the two ladies and said, "You should think your project over again, Señorita, when you've calmed down, or else you might regret it!"

"Don't you worry about me, Herr von Lichtenau," she answered pertly.

Lichtenau left the dining hall and walked out onto the deck, stopping at the ship's rail and looking out over the sea, which was much calmer now. "Silly little girl!" he thought. He felt some anger well up inside him, but as he stood there, gazing into the distance, somebody gently touched his arm. He turned around and found himself looking into Juanita's dark eyes. Very softly and somewhat hesitatingly her lips formed the words, "Don't be angry with me, Herr von Lichtenau! Was I misbehaving too much?"

"Just a little unreasonably, Señorita."

The accommodating tone of his voice restored her self-assurance, inducing her to add excitedly, "You must believe me! I am genuinely interested in your research work. Does that really sound so far-fetched? But you see, I'd love to get into a serious activity of some kind." And a little distressed she added: "My life is so empty—I realized that in a profound way as I was listening to you talk about your own aspirations. Let me come with you as your assistant!" She gestured imploringly to lend greater emphasis to her words.

"It's really not possible, Señorita."

Clearly disappointed, Juanita was at the point of tears and her full lips were trembling. Lichtenau said soothingly: "Impossible. At least for the time being." And he started to describe in detail the hardships and difficulties that would be facing him and which he would have to surmount to reach his goal. He spoke to her in his usual quiet manner and gradually she began to grasp the fact that she could not be of any use to him at present; but when he promised to write to her as soon as his expedition was over, her face lit up. She grasped his hand; "I take your word for it; I'll be waiting."

"That you may, Señorita. I am glad to see that you understand. I am going to report to you in Mexico City, regularly."

Having sealed the promise with a handshake, they stood side by side in total silence, their respective thoughts and emotions speaking in a wordless language of their own. More than in any previous exchange, it was this shared silence that seemed to bind them together. Finally, directing her dark eyes up to his once again—Juanita said: "I'll have to go now, Herr von Lichtenau, it's getting cool."

Lichtenau turned toward her. His gaze enveloped her and she blushed slightly.

"Well then, Señorita, let's look forward to a nice friendship! Tomorrow morning we'll put into port and there our path will diverge for the moment. But I am beginning to think that they will merge again one day."

He bent down, took her small hand and kissed it.

"Good bye then, Herr von Lichtenau!" she cried with a happy smile and ran off to her cabin. Lichtenau was alone.

The next day the ship arrived at his destination on the Yucatan coast and Lichtenau had reached his intermediate goal. He bid Señorita Juanita farewell. She was quiet and reserved; only her eyes spoke to him of her true feelings. Once more he thanked her warmly for her concern and repeated his promise to write soon.

"It will please me to hear from you," she said in a cool and conventional manner while holding out her hand. But then her feelings broke through the barriers of social restraint, her eyes grew moist and she hesitated: "You will call me to your side soon won't you? May the Holy Virgin protect you and...." She stopped abruptly. Her words, not unlike an imploring plea, touched his heart. "Dear little girl," he thought. Once more his gaze enveloped her slender figure with heart-felt emotion, his sinewy hand clasped hers even more firmly, and he said: "We shall meet again, Señorita, I know it, I can feel it inside."

A flash of light in her dark eyes showed her gratitude.

"Good bye, Señorita!"

"Good bye, Herr von Lichtenau!" Juanita's voice was full of cheer again.

Lichtenau politely bowed to Señora Dolores, who had been observing the scene in icy silence and merely responded with a short nod. The young people's eyes met for the last time—then Lichtenau turned and headed for the ship's ladder, leading down to the launch which would take him ashore.

Once ashore he was met by the customary bustle of a busy Mexican port. He was immediately surrounded by several swarthy fellows, clad in the local variegated dress and with huge sombreros on their heads, each of them trying to out-do the others by shouting and waving their arms in an attempt to promote the hotels for which they had come to find guests. Lichtenau looked from one to the other with amusement. Eventually, he signaled to the one who appeared to be the most trustworthy. At once the fellow picked up the young man's luggage, carried it to a shabby looking carriage waiting nearby, and after a short ride they reached the hotel where Lichtenau was given a spacious room with windows offering an expansive view of the ocean. After a full lunch, just a trifle too spicy for his taste, Lichtenau spent a few hours bent over his books. Toward evening, when the heat of the day had abated somewhat, he went out for a stroll about town. He was looking for a reliable guide and some horses for the upcoming adventure and he knew that this task would not be easy in a foreign country like this; earlier experience had taught him to be extremely cautious.

After a considerable time meandering about town, the search took him into one of the many taverns near the harbor. He let his gaze glide over all the brazen-faced fellows sitting around tables, gambling with dice, drinking and holding raucous conversations. The young German went up to the bar and ordered some wine; when he had finished his drink, he turned to leave but at the door he bumped into a young man wearing moccasins like the local Indians but with light skin and straight black hair that indicated one of mixed heritage, known locally as a Mestizo. He had intense piercing eyes and his lips were closed tightly. The two men's eyes met for a moment—then the Mexican stepped into the tavern, threw his sombrero onto an empty table, slowly untied the kerchief he was wearing around his neck and sat down.

Unable to decide what to do, Lichtenau remained standing in the doorway. There was something he liked about this young man and so he finally went back into the bar and joined him at his table. Paying no attention to Lichtenau at all, the Mestizo lit his pipe, called for wine, and gave himself up to his thoughts. Lichtenau could not take his eyes off him as the fellow attracted him more and more. Eventually, having wondered for some time how to strike up a conversation, he pulled himself together and

without further hesitation asked: "Excuse me, Señor, could you tell me where I might find a guide and some horses to get to the old Indian villages in the area of the Mayan ruins?" The native turned his head in surprise. Lichtenau felt the intense, penetrating stare of those raven-black eyes and then the man said in a heavy accent: "The Señor can buy horses anywhere and, as for the guide, I will take you to those ruins. Fact is, I come from up there...." Lichtenau felt relieved. He had not expected to reach his goal so quickly. Restraining himself however, he asked calmly: "How long will it take us to get to Telchaquillo?"
The man thought about it briefly. "With good horses, just a few days. I've already acted as a guide to other people who wanted to go up there. It's not an undertaking one could call entirely safe; there are bandits hanging around in those hills, but I have what it takes!" he said, tapping slightly against the holster of a gun hanging from his belt. Then he added: "The innkeeper here knows me. You need not worry about me!"

Lichtenau sank back in thought, once in a while casting a scrutinizing glance at the Mestizo. Then he said:

"Very well. I shall think about it. Report to Señora Margarita at the Casa d'Orfeo tomorrow." He got up, handed the man some advance money and went out to the street.

Paolo Samblo remained seated after Lichtenau had left. He took one of the coins he had just received and decided to inquire into the future by flipping it. If it came up heads, the foreign señor would take him along. "Holy Virgin!" he whispered, "it's heads!" Visibly delighted, Paolo put the coin back into his pocket, paid his bill at the bar, and set out to find some horses.

Back at his hotel, Lichtenau went up to his room at once; he took out his many plans and written notes and buried himself in his studies. He was painfully aware that he still hadn't come anywhere near Atlantis, the land of his dreams. In Peru he had searched the Incas' temples in every detail, but without success. With a sigh he put his papers back into their case.

The following morning the Mestizo arrived on time. He informed Lichtenau that he had found suitable horses and Lichtenau decided to entrust the man with the preparations for their small expedition.

The next day Paolo came back early in the morning, bringing with him three strong horses and other necessary equipment, including tents and all manner of additional gear. Lichtenau was satisfied; Paolo had proven himself to be reliable, Lichtenau told him so, and—to add weight to his words—Lichtenau handed him more money. The Mestizo's pleasure showed on his radiant face as he reassured Lichtenau of his loyalty.

"When can we start?" Lichtenau asked, interrupting the man's outburst.

"If the Señor desires so, in one hour—then we'll reach the forest leading up to the high plateau by lunch time."

"And where do we proceed from there?"

"The ruins you wish to see are on that high plateau!"

"Very well, Paolo. In one hour." Lichtenau held out his hand to the Mestizo who was clearly flattered by this gesture and returned the handshake with such force that Lichtenau had difficulty holding back a cry of pain.

They sat out on their journey at the appointed time. Soon the town was well behind them and they entered a steppe-like region. They continued riding for a long time before the landscape eventually changed to scrub and then to a dense forest. Following a narrow trail, they proceeded through a dimly-lit thicket. Fallen trees and the wild, overgrown underbrush slowed down their progress considerably. Eventually they were enveloped by a warm, humid mist as their horses snorted nervously. Green, iridescent lizards darted across their path, fixing their gaze on the men for an instant before quickly disappearing into the bushes.

Multicolored birds could be seen flitting about in the sun-streaked twilight and swarms of playful, whirling insects filled the sunny spots between the trees. It was only after many more hours of travel that they came to the edge of the jungle and found themselves once more under the relentless eye of the bright Mexican sun. An expansive and weather-beaten treeless slope appeared before them. Paolo pointed to a narrow line undulating upward:

"Do you see that trail, Señor? It's leading up to the high plateau of Mayapan." Lichtenau followed the trail up through his binoculars. His white tropical clothing was drenched with perspiration. "It is hot and I am tired. Let us get some rest, Paolo," he said as he lowered his binoculars.

The willing guide brought everything they needed within reach and they quickly settled in shade of the age-old trees at the edge of the forest. As they enjoyed some of the food they had brought with them, Lichtenau could not stop observing the Mestizo: How lithe and supple he was, resembling a rare animal of prey! The outline of his brown face was sharp, two deeply cut lines framed his full-lipped mouth, reflecting a life which had certainly not been easy. Lichtenau asked him abruptly: "Are you married?" "No," Paolo answered gruffly, a hard glint appeared in his eyes and the sharp lines around his mouth deepened. Lichtenau sensed that he had touched a sore spot. "Don't worry, Paolo! Same here! I haven't found the right one yet either. But it's better to wait than to pick the wrong one," he said appeasingly.

Paolo said nothing for a moment and then when he finally did speak Lichtenau detected a slight tremor in his voice: "I *had* found the right one, but another, a foreign man, took her away from me. He was rich and Paolo was poor." A menacing spark flashed up in his eyes, when he added with an angry hiss, "I loath foreigners!" Lichtenau started to feel uncomfortable; he rose to his feet, allowing his hand to move toward his gun holster but Paolo laughed out loud and said: "Don't worry, Señor! You are a good man! You shook hands with Paolo—so, Paolo will always serve and protect you against any one—no matter who!"

Lichtenau was perplexed by this sudden shift in the man's mood. He managed a forced smile. "Strange fellow," he thought, "speaking of hate and fondness for foreigners in the same breath."

"Time to move on, Paolo!"

Carefully testing the ground with their hooves, the horses continued to struggle up the narrow and often steep trail. The sun was still burning mercilessly and though it took considerable effort by both the animals and the two men, they finally reached the high plateau where the horses stopped, snorting.

Before the two men lay an immense plain, covered with dried grass and stretching as far as the eye could see, with the bizarre shape of an occasional cactus reaching up toward the sky. In the far distance, tiny huts appeared through the high grass and Lichtenau motioned to Paolo that he had noticed the village.

"That's where we are headed, Señor. It's a Mestizo hamlet; we're going to stay there for the night."

They rode on at a swift pace now and by the time they reached the small village, consisting of a few poor huts, the moon had already risen. It was immediately clear that Paolo knew his way around this place and as soon as he had called out, life began to stir within the buildings. Men and women came out into the open from all directions and stared at the travelers. Paolo exchanged a few words with them and soon an old man with white hair—apparently the elder of the village—came up to them. He lifted his shabby sombrero in brief greeting to Lichtenau. When Paolo had explained what he and Lichtenau wanted, the elder said: "You are welcome to stay and spend the night in my house"—and turning to his people, he added: "The stranger is my guest."

This pronouncement broke the spell as the men crowded around Lichtenau. Each one of them had a few friendly words to say and the young German scholar answered in his usual friendly manner. "Thank you for your hospitality. Tomorrow morning I will repay your kindness as best I can but now we must get some sleep, we are very tired."

He dismounted and followed the elder into a hut where he was given a simple straw mattress and a resting place for the night. Paolo remained outside with the horses which he tied up, then he squatted down beside them with his legs crossed, and spent the night leaning his back against the side of the shack.

The sun's radiant majesty was already blazing from the cloudless sky above them when Lichtenau politely took his leave from his host, handed him and the other villagers some coins, which were accepted with thanks, and moved on as the desolate wilderness swallowed up the two horsemen once again.

They allowed themselves only brief stopovers in the scanty shade of the few large cacti along their way and moved on quickly afterwards. Having traveled in this fashion for several days, spending their nights in various Mestizo villages, they finally arrived at a vantage point from where they could distinguish a darkish rise in the ground near the horizon. As they approached more closely and using his binoculars, Lichtenau was able to identify it as the ruins of Mayapan.

However, one more overnight stay in a village was needed before they were able to make out the impressive remnants of the primitive wall surrounding the ancient Mayan capital. It was around midday and Lichtenau was immediately overcome with feverish expectation. He pressed Paolo to proceed faster and soon they were racing their horses across the shimmering plain and under a scorching sun. Their horses were covered with sweat and foam as Lichtenau fell victim to a sudden, leaden, fatigue in all his limbs. The sweltering heat was clearly getting the better of him and he had to struggle with all his willpower to remain in possession of his senses. Perspiration was streaming down his now-ghostly face. His breathing had become difficult and spasmodic when he suddenly felt giddy, bent forward over his horse's neck, and collapsed with a deep groan. After a few more paces the horse stood motionless.

When Paolo became aware of Lichtenau's condition, he rushed to his side, jumping down from his horse just in time to catch the young scholar in his arms. Then, laying him on the ground as comfortably as possible, he opened his shirt and tried to cool him by fanning some air over him with his sombrero. After a short while Lichtenau opened his eyes. With great effort he sat up a little but instantly sank back again while Paolo looked on anxiously. Then the Mestizo had an idea. He walked over to his horse and took a small vial from his saddle-bag which he opened and put to Lichtenau's lips: "Drink this, Señor, it will do you good!"

Lichtenau drank eagerly—and almost immediately all fatigue and heaviness vanished from his limbs. Wide awake and feeling like a new man, he stretched happily and stood up with a jump.

"I suppose that was a magic potion or something?"

"No, Señor," said Paolo and smiled. "That's not what it was. Just wine with a few drops of peyote in it, a poison made from a small thornless cactus of the same name, a plant that looks something like a pebble, actually. But one has to be careful in using it; if it's not taken in the right way, one may lose one's mind or even die."

"Peyote!" Lichtenau vaguely remembered having read about it, and climbing back up into his saddle he said cheerfully: "At any rate, thank you, Paolo! This heat really wore me out. But now let's go on! I want to get to the ruins before nightfall."

The powerful city wall was looming closer and closer until—finally—there it was! Lichtenau decided to ride along the wall in search of an appropriate spot to set up camp. Eventually he chose a small cleft in the wall with a few cacti nearby. Paolo's first concern was with the horses. He rubbed them down with great care and gave them some water from the water bag they had carried with them; then he put up the tent. Lichtenau sank down onto his blanket with a sigh of relief: "Whew—what a murderous heat!" he said stretching out on his back.

Paolo slipped into the tent without making a sound and squatted down beside Lichtenau.

"Do you still want to see the ruins today, Señor?"

"Tomorrow morning, Paolo. It will be better to get some rest first."

The Mestizo nodded in agreement. Suddenly, his expression changed and sat motionless, gazing in front of him with a fixed stare.

"What's wrong, Paolo?" asked Lichtenau who had noticed the change in Paolo's face. The Mestizo mumbled a few incomprehensible words in a monotone. What was the matter with the fellow? Lichtenau rose up a little. Paolo's eyes were wide open as he sat there staring into the empty space before him and it was as if he *saw* something while repeating the same unintelligible sounds over and over again. Lichtenau tapped him slightly on the shoulder. The Mestizo jolted, his eyes no longer fixated, his features relaxed.

"What did you see, Paolo?" Lichtenau urged him.

The Mestizo looked around with apprehension, then whispered: "The ghosts of Mayapan are watching over this holy place, Señor. We must try to appease their anger if we do not want to pay with our lives."

"Primitive superstition," Lichtenau thought, in his initial urge to dismiss Paolo's appeal, but then decided to say nothing. He remembered the slow and insidious death of a well-known scholar and his assistant following their entering an Egyptian burial chamber. At the time, even the most renowned doctors had been unable to establish the cause of their death. The burial chamber had also been examined meticulously. Any hypothesis that the two men had died of an infection caused by insects or because of some mysterious poisonous substances, perhaps painted on the walls of the burial chamber, had proven incorrect. The case had been taken up by the international press and discussed at great length; the most far-fetched conjectures had been proposed—even going so far as to suggest that the priests of Ancient Egypt had induced the mysterious deaths by means of special magic powers which they had "cast" upon that place in order to protect the tombs against subsequent intruders. Could it be that similar dangers were lurking here, too? As he had been brought up to think along lines of modern rationality, Lichtenau's mind always rejected any suggestion by which the deaths in Egypt could be called "mysterious." He was aware, however, that such an attitude did not provide him with an explanation either. For the first time he allowed himself to wonder whether this simple man was not closer to the facts by his faith than academically enlightened scientists. On his many journeys, undertaken to follow the vestiges of ancient peoples, Lichtenau had encountered mystery after mystery, all as yet unsolved. And each time, he had had to accept this fact with a shrug. It had probably been no more than his own imagination, self-delusion, or auto-suggestive tendencies that had sometimes made him believe in "mysteries," he figured, and in the same way Paolo must, no doubt, be suffering from hallucinations and must be seeing as real something that was nothing more than imagination. Still, some faint, uncomfortable feeling about these things always remained—a feeling the young scholar found he could not entirely put aside. Now, too, he struggled against this feeling with all the tools of his logical mind—and he struggled until sleep eventually overtook him.

When he woke up the next morning, Paolo was already standing fully dressed by the side of his bed. Lichtenau refreshed himself with what they could spare of their water. During breakfast Paolo said that he had already been doing some scouting around. "Through that hole in the wall we can get as far as the Temple of the Sun," he said. Lichtenau listened with interest.

"All right, Paolo, we shall try."

So after they broke camp Paolo led his horse carefully through the gap in the wall and Lichtenau followed, leading his horse after him. They came upon a vast field strewn with stones and debris of all shapes and sizes. Moving cautiously around the obstacles, they walked their horses up to a large, rather dilapidated flight of open stairs that had originally been built by fitting together huge square stones.

There was nothing special to be seen anywhere. Slowly Lichtenau rode along the foot of the stairs, then turned around the corner at the far end of the temple—there, too, he had to navigate around stone blocks, rubble, and cacti. It was the scholar in him that prompted him to study the ancient wall where, all of a sudden, he noticed a wide, dark crevice at a level well above the height of a grown man and which looked man-made. He called to Paolo: "Do you see that hole up there? We must try to get inside the temple from there. Set the tent up and fasten the horses!"

Paolo obeyed quietly while Lichtenau checked his revolver and flashlight, telling Paolo to do the same. Then Paolo—carrying a machete, an ax and a rope—followed the young German to the foot of the temple wall. He climbed onto Paolo's shoulders and pulled himself up into the opening. Paolo followed, pulling himself up by the rope Lichtenau had thrown down to him. Carefully, step by step the two of them penetrated the dark passageway. The light of their flashlights suddenly illuminated a low narrow corridor leading downward in spiral-like turns and apparently directed toward the inner part of the building. There were other tunnels coming from both sides and crossing their path.

The two men tried to maintain the general direction of their progress but this proved a difficult thing to do, especially when their path suddenly branched off into a whole series of different tunnels at once. Lichtenau stood silently, not knowing which path to choose.

"It looks like the Maze of the Minotaur was modeled after this," he whispered nervously to himself.

Paolo stepped up to him. He had been walking behind Lichtenau with some apprehension. Lizards scurrying by and other creeping things had stimulated his imagination. He asked in a low and somewhat fearful voice: "Do you really wish to continue, Señor? We might get lost in here and starve to death!"

The fear in this strong muscular fellow actually made the explorer laugh—indeed, it actually gave him more confidence. He said: "We'll go on, Paolo. We haven't seen anything so far that is of particular interest to me. But—quiet!" He fell silent and strained to hear. "Do you hear anything?"

Paolo listened. "I can hear some noise—it sounds like the distant murmur of water," he said.

"We'll check it out! Let's go!" Lichtenau turned into the tunnel from which the noise seemed to be coming. Soon this corridor narrowed considerably and became so low that the two men had to bend down sharply to be able to proceed on their way. The noise of splashing water increased with every step and grew loudest as the tunnel widened into a small cave. They let the beam of their flashlights move across the walls—and discovered a startling array of hieroglyphs. They could hear water splashing in the far corner of the cave. When they had moved closer, it was possible to make out a sculptured stone basin, the rim of which was embellished with intertwining ornaments that ended with animal heads.

A thought occurred to Lichtenau. "Do you think you could find your way back alone?" he asked Paolo.

"I think I could, Señor."

"In that case, go back and fetch our water bags so there won't be any water problem for us later."

The Mestizo hesitated, then he replied: "You can't stay here by yourself, Señor! If anything should happen to you, nobody would be here to help you."

"What are you afraid could happen to me, Paolo? There is no one here—at least no human beings—and as for your ghosts—well, I think I can cope," Lichtenau said with a smile.

Paolo made the sign of the cross upon his chest and walked away, as the soft sound of his footsteps faded quickly in the distance.

Lichtenau was alone. As he began to inspect the hieroglyphs by flashlight he noticed the recurring image of a bird, above which was a blazing sun disc sending forth its rays. In between these symbols were vertical and horizontal lines, but also undulating ones—and between these, a closed eye and the outline of a lower jaw.

At the sight of these images the young scholar sank deep into thought. Soon, however, he felt sure of the meaning of these various symbols. He had read about them in the researchers' books on the Mayan script: the bird was the mythological bird Moan and probably stood for the human soul, the sun disc was Yaxin, the main god worshipped here, while the closed eye coupled with the fleshless jaw symbolized Cimi, Death.

As Lichtenau kept moving along the wall, the entrance of a new tunnel suddenly opened before him. As he entered, he noticed that the general pattern remained the same as before: as the path lead downward in sinewy turns, many new tunnels opened into it. As though drawn forward by some unknown force, Lichtenau continued to walk. Could it be that the knowledge he had been searching for all these years was awaiting him in *this* place...?

His path cut through many intermediate smaller and larger caves and their walls were covered with hieroglyphic engravings as well, amongst which birds, the sun and eyes could be recognized over and over again.

Lichtenau glanced at his watch. Good God! Hours had passed since he entered this world of meandering pathways. Suddenly an inner voice warned him to go back, but he disregarded these whispers from his soul and he continued on. Just then he was startled by the impression of having already been in this or that cave. "I have lost my way," flashed through his mind, paralyzing him, as he stopped and began to think. He would simply have to go back—he could use the imprints of his own footsteps to lead him out! As he carefully observed the ground in the light of his torch, he walked back slowly—but soon the traces of his feet became intermingled, the tunnel forked in many directions and he could see footprints going everywhere. Which was the right direction? Uneasy sensations began to take hold of him. Again he stopped. He called Paolo. The echo of his voice came back many times but no answer from his companion. He turned into another tunnel, with the faint hope of finding his way back from there. He started running...on and on he ran, but he never once saw daylight ahead.

Eventually the tunnel widened and Lichtenau stepped into a large subterranean chamber, the walls of which were covered with sculptured images cut in strong relief, and at once the scholar's interest made him forget the dangerous situation he was in. He could make out an amazing pair of sculptured effigies, each of which showed a pair of human beings with smooth and harmonious features. He moved beyond these sculptured likenesses and moved deeper into the grotto. Here he found a semicircular area, elevated somewhat above the entrance to the chamber, that could be reached by a number of steps hewn into the very granite of the cave.

Suddenly Lichtenau became aware of the statue of a man, sitting with his back towards him, in the center of that elevated part of the chamber. He walked up the steps to get a closer look as he began wondering whether he saw correctly or if he was being fooled by his senses: the statue was wrapped in a dull-colored cloak that seemed to be made of cloth. The beam of his flashlight told him that he was not mistaken! The statue *was* clad in a large coat of woven material. Lichtenau went closer to look at the statue from the front and saw an age-old face covered by a dense network of wrinkles and creases. The statue's head was covered with a handkerchief folded in an unusual fashion and held on by a headband. Lichtenau stood motionless and stared at the mysterious statue's face; but then, he wondered...was it a statue or a mummy? "If it is a mummy," he thought, "I must not touch it lest it crumbles into dust." He brought his flashlight still closer to that face. The "statue" seemed to be breathing—or was that an optical illusion? The scholar was of two minds: Should he or shouldn't he touch the "man?"

Not sure what to do, Lichtenau stood for a long time—then, having made his decision, he stretched out his hand to touch the figure...but at precisely that moment it opened its eyes! Startled, Lichtenau moved back a step. "A human being?" he thought, when a deep and pleasant voice addressed him: "Have you finally found your way back home, Nabor, Lucoman of the Mayan Empire?"

Lichtenau was awestruck as he stood staring into two large eyes that shone with fascinating brilliance and were looking at him with a deep kindness. Lichtenau recovered slowly from his shock and finally managed to ask in a troubled voice, "Forgive me, but I don't understand the meaning of your words."

A smile brought life to the wrinkled face of the old man: "You have been away for a long time, Nabor! Since the day you turned away from *Elohim*, the Great Spirit of Light, the rebellious believer you had become has had to walk many a painful road through the millennia."

The voice fell silent. Lichtenau thought he must be dreaming! A human being in this solitary place, deep below the ground— and calling him Nabor and claiming to have been waiting for him! Surely, he must be having hallucinations. "Perhaps this man is demented," Lichtenau thought. "I am not going to get involved.... On the other hand, this old man must know his way about in this maze and will be able to help me find my way out," he pondered. So, he asked in a loud voice: "You called me 'Nabor', old man, didn't you? 'Nabor'? Right? All right, I used to be your

Nabor, but tell me more! It's been so long and I have forgotten so many things."

"Don't you ridicule my words, Nabor! This is not the time for it," replied the old man in earnest dignity, and when he rose to his feet it became clear that he was taller than Lichtenau by as much as a head's length. His kind gaze enveloped the young man and somehow seemed to calm his inner turmoil. Lichtenau stammered in embarrassment: "I'm confused by your words, words which I am unable to fathom."

The old man nodded gently and beckoned to Lichtenau to follow him. Walking slowly, this perplexing individual preceded the young German to the far end of the cave, where he bent down a little and entered a tunnel. There he turned to Lichtenau and said: "Switch off your artificial light, Nabor! You don't need it here. Just keep close to me, then nothing will happen to you."

Lichtenau did as he was told and turned off his flashlight. At first he sank into darkness but soon he was able to see the old man in front of him, surrounded by a soft luminescence. They continued walking. By now, Lichtenau had certainly become captive to this extraordinary adventure; he felt safe and as if filled with a joyous expectation—and he somehow couldn't help but feel amused at himself.

Again the path was meandering along. Eventually the old man stopped. When Lichtenau came up to him, he saw that his guide was—quite effortlessly, it seemed—prying a large stone out of the wall and rolling it to the side, creating a new entrance. The old man disappeared into the opening and Lichtenau followed. Again they proceeded—but only for a short while, for at last the tunnel seemed to have come to an end.

The old man pushed aside a heavy curtain and Lichtenau found himself looking into a spacious apartment where he was able to distinguish various pieces of furniture, all lit by some undefined iridescent light. He stopped and looked at his guide in surprise.

"Step inside, Nabor! *Elohim*'s blessing be with you!"

Moving past the old man, Lichtenau walked into the room. His immediate impression was that of entering a dream state.

The walls of the high room were made of polished stones, similar to opals, and precious carpets and animal skins covered the floor; along the walls stood broad sofas on feet shaped in the Greek style. There were also armchairs without backs, as they had been fashioned in Greek antiquity; a number of round marble tables completed the picture.

Lichtenau just stood and stared, barely daring to breath, all the while fearing the beautiful vision might dissolve into nothing. The old man's voice broke into his preoccupation, "Take a seat, Nabor!"—and he pointed to a chair. Lichtenau seated himself, hesitating a little, his eyes still riveted by the fantastic splendor about him.

The old man walked over to one of the corners of the apartment and returned with a dish made of agate and filled with a crystal-clear liquid. This he put down before the young man who—after taking a sip—moved the cup away from his lips and asked: "Old man, what are you offering me here?"

"Just spring water to which were added some herbs!"

Questions welled up inside Lichtenau's mind, but he was too shy to ask them out loud. By now the old man was seated on one of the sofas opposite, as Lichtenau looked at him expectantly. When the old man finally spoke, he said: "You have veered off the right track considerably, Nabor, since I last saw you."

"And when might that have been?"

"For you, thousands of years ago; for me—it was yesterday."

Lichtenau stared at the old man incredulously but conscious that gazing into those eyes in that sallow face was like looking into the depths of space. Indeed, those eyes held him as if by a magic spell, their steady gaze penetrating his very being down to the most profound reaches of his soul. And again he heard the old man's deep voice speaking: "Your soul is as old as the world. Your path started at its very beginning. You experienced many other worlds before setting foot on this continent. It is the land which you have set out to discover in this life, the country that had already filled the dreams of your boyhood."

"So, it was in—Atlantis?" Lichtenau interrupted in excitement.

"That's right. In Eya-Eya, the blessed island of which the myths of humanity still give some blurred reflection." The old man fell silent. His wrinkled face resembled a death-mask, but then it became lively again: His eyelids lifted and his puzzling eyes shone brighter even than before. He said: "Your great thirst for knowledge of these things made you set out on this journey. But these things are already in you, though dormant, and have been accompanying you through many lives. For you must know that your soul keeps constantly moving through life after life."

Lichtenau sat deeply in thought. Indeed, had there not been instances in which he felt that he had already walked many roads on this planet? Often during the hours of the night his mind had been crowded by images he didn't understand and which he had mostly forgotten in the morning. Could it be that the doctrine of reincarnation was telling the truth?

The old man cut short these ruminations, "It is the truth!"

Lichtenau looked up in astonishment; his critical reasoning mind objected, "Then one can be reincarnated back into the animal kingdom, as it is taught in India?"

"No! The mineral realm, the realm of the animals and that of man are strictly separated from one another. The animals have younger souls, souls that must undergo a different kind of transformation; thousands of animal souls correspond to one human soul."

The young scholar fought his doubts—all the more as the old man's calm and determined manner presented these ideas with such utter conviction that it was now even harder for him to deny them.

"All I want is to help you recover your lost knowledge, Nabor! Just look at the water! In the cycles of nature it turns to mist first, then moves upward only to be bound into clouds—and comes down again in the form of raindrops—that is to say, water, meant to continue this circulatory movement in all eternity. Similarly, the beings of this Earth continue to move in a circuit in the course of which they de-incarnate and move to another realm from whence they return to incarnate again. Only a few individuals can break this circuit by using their minds to push up toward the Light."

"That other realm—where is it? I never saw it."

"Your consciousness is dimmed, Nabor! You hold yourself a prisoner to the image-building of this world. Return to yourself! Stop the foreign voices chatting away inside you and listen to the voice of your own spirit!"

"I've tried, old man; I meditated and I pondered but often I thought this to be a vain effort. My reasoning power proved a failure every time and I had no idea what to do about it."

Lichtenau felt a sudden urge to speak to this strange man in detail, to spread out before him the past few years of his life with all the ups and downs of his hopes and disappointments. The old man listened quietly, his gaze unswervingly fixed on the young scholar who, finally, broke off with a hopeless shrug of his shoulders.

"Because it does not have a light of its own, the reason of man often goes astray," the old man said. "Simply start to live again as you used to, Nabor; in all things ask the spirit inside you, your best friend. You can never lose your way if you entrust yourself to its guidance."

"You mean the voice of my conscience?"

"That voice is an emanation of mental rays. Whenever you have the intention of doing something wrong, you will realize how your inner calm is lost. This is the sign of your mind warning you. The soul has its seat between the navel and the stomach—hence the discomfort when one does not act in compliance with one's inner laws. This discomfort is a warning signal: it goes to the cerebellum and from there to the cerebrum, as well as to the abdomen. The brain is our regulatory system and depends on psychological impulses."

"What is the difference between spirit and soul?" Lichtenau asked.

"The spirit is the being as such; it is enveloped by the soul whose outer sheath is the body."

"In that case, there should be another world!"

"Correct! You need the body for your earthly existence but you will shed it at the time of your physical death and remain in your soul-body in the world of souls, the twilight kingdom. When you have freed yourself from all worldly attachment, you will also cast off the soul-body and enter, as a spirit, the light-filled world of the Spirit. All these realms still belong to the Earth's aura, however."

"Does this aura correspond to an extension of the Earth's own fields of energy?"

"Yes. Each planet has its own aura. The planets touch each other at the outer limits of their respective auras, thus forming one single whole. Also, each human being has his or her own aura." Noticing Lichtenau's questioning eyes, he added: "The aura is the radiation of the soul's content, the radiation of your own personal energy— an energy we possess in the same way our globe possesses it. This energy surrounds us and reinforces our psychic radiation. When this psychic radiation becomes strong enough to cause the energy belt around us to burst, it is as if a light were switched on in a dark room that we had entered but where we had not, to that point, been able to recognize anything. But then all of a sudden, in the new light, we're able to see all the things around us with perfect clarity. The darkness in which you are still abiding now will also be illuminated one day, through the energy belt around you."

Lichtenau was confounded by what he heard. He recalled the faint luminescence he had seen around the old man's tall figure earlier, the luminescence which had also lit the path they had walked along together in the dark tunnel. Remembering this, it suddenly struck him that a long time must have passed since that observation. He glanced at his watch. It had stopped. With a surly expression in his eyes, he looked up, encountering a delicate smile around the old man's mouth.

"Your watch is unable to withstand the atmosphere in this room. But you should not worry about that, Nabor! Time does not prevail here. You have stepped out into the timelessness of the Cosmos and you will return to the world of man after your initiation has been completed."

"But Paolo will be looking for me!" Lichtenau insisted.

"Let him! There's a lot he has to make up for as far as you are concerned," came the mysterious answer.

Again Lichtenau was yielding to his brooding suspicions; his previous distrust had come back. He knew he was in the old man's power and he also realized that the sage was intent on keeping him here for some time.

"Don't torment yourself, Nabor! You are my guest. Are you not here under my protection of your own free will?" Then he added, "But now it's time for your body to take some rest."

Lichtenau nodded, for suddenly he had become aware of a leaden fatigue engulfing him. Only with great effort did he manage to get up and to move over to the couch and stretch out, as directed by the old man. The old man had also closed his eyes; his face seemed as rigid as a mummy's. But for Lichtenau's breathing, a deep silence had settled in the room.

Lichtenau was dreaming. He saw the old man's face before him, he saw his entire figure standing there taller even than in reality. A long white gown flowed around him and on his head he wore a high headdress from which a white cloth fell down to his shoulders. His face was that of an old man, framed by a beard as white as snow.

The vision spoke to him in some unintelligible language and seemed to be reproaching him for something. He tried to defend himself. At that moment the sage's face turned hard and severe, his eyes were flashing like bolts of lightning. The threatening image came closer and closer. Lichtenau began groaning in his sleep. Again the old man's face changed. This time it took on a humble expression which was emphasized further by the pleading gesture of his hands.

Lichtenau awoke. For a while the dream vision kept him enthralled, then he grew conscious of his surroundings. Raising himself, he looked around. Now he remembered! He turned his head, searching for the old man. In vain; he was alone. He jumped to his feet. What was the meaning of all this? He went up to the heavy curtain and thrust it back: There before him stood the old sage holding a large dish in his hands. To Lichtenau's surprise it was filled with pastries and a variety of fruit. The old man placed the dish on the table and then he even produced fresh drinks.

"Eat and drink, Lucoman!" he invited Lichtenau.

The young scholar served himself with some hesitation but the food was so delicious that he soon forgot all restraint and

prudence. He ate with great appetite while the old sage kept his watchful eyes on him. Aware of his gaze, Lichtenau asked:
"Why don't you eat anything, old man?"
"I am no longer in need of earthly food."
"How can that be?" Lichtenau asked, much taken aback.
"*Elohim*'s radiating power sustains my mortal frame," he replied.
"Unthinkable," Lichtenau reflected. Was it not obvious that the old man, too, was a human being of flesh and blood? Of course, there were yogis in India said to dwell in Himalayan caves who kept their bodies alive for centuries without any intake of food. In the past he had rejected such statements outright as belonging to the realm of fantasy, but now he began to wonder whether the old man was not, after all, speaking the truth....

"Have you forgotten, Nabor, that you are a spark of the spirit of *Elohim*, Father of all?"

What could one say to that? The old man continued:

"That spirit is wrapped in a sheath of electromagnetic energy similar in aspect to your external body, so when you become one with your own internal spirit, its light will flood into all the different parts of your soul and enter all and every cell of your physical frame. When the Eternal One ascends to power within you, you will never again feel hungry or thirsty, nor cold nor tired."

There! The old man's face underwent yet another transformation, now looking at once visibly younger with his eyes emitting a profusion of light and his entire figure beaming forth an incandescent glow. He stood there surrounded by a shining cloud from which flame-shaped beams of light went off in all directions. This light was soon engulfing Lichtenau also, whereupon he clearly felt that his bodily heaviness had completely disappeared. An all-encompassing sensation of bliss rose up inside him as he kept gazing into those radiating eyes; he felt liberated from his Ego and abandoned himself entirely to the irradiating influence of the old man's extraordinary being. All his desires were suppressed, no thoughts disturbed him, he barely noticed his own breathing.

Then the face of his host returned to normal—the radiating luminescence dimmed away and only his eyes continued to hold that enrapturing glow. In a very low voice the old man said, "Do you realize now, Nabor, what you lost when you turned away from *Elohim*, losing your faith in Him and in yourself?"

Lichtenau remained silent. His adventure had thoroughly shaken him.

"Do you believe me now, Nabor?"

Lichtenau nodded, but said nothing.

"Your thirst for knowledge has driven you hither and thither in this world, but wherever you were searching you found no more than what others had discovered before you."

Again Lichtenau nodded, a sad expression obscuring his features.

"You ought to realize, Nabor, that the external desire for such knowledge was only an inner longing inspired by your spirit's wish to return home to the bright world of its origin. We met one another often on the roads of this world, but you did not recognize me. Your inner eye was closed. Even during this life of yours I have been around you many times, invisible to your earthly eyes, and Lehuana assisted me in kindling the thirst for knowledge within you and fanning your dedication into flame."

"Lehuana?" Lichtenau asked.

"She was the Lucoman of the Raya Empire who provided you with the physical body of your incarnation as Nabor and your physical body for this life as well."

"Then she was my mother!" Lichtenau cried in dismay.

"That's right. She is here with us, now! Just close your eyes and free yourself from all thoughts—then you will recognize her and hear her voice."

A supernatural silence spread around them. Lichtenau closed his eyes and soon noticed a figure, made of light and surrounded by an amazing aura, standing beside the old sage and directly in front of him. At first he was unable to make out anything concrete in that shining halo but then outlines began to appear—and then…he saw his mother's face. Love and kindness were radiating forth at him when he heard her voice saying: "Erik, do trust in Huatami! He stayed back in the earthly world because of you. He wants to guide you back because he rejected you once." His mother's figure moved closer; her brightly shining hand gently stroked his head. It felt like a soft summer breeze caressing him. Then the apparition faded, leaving behind only a phosphorescent glow of light. Gradually this too died away, leaving the young scholar deeply shaken. He opened his eyes. Both men remained silent for a long time. Not a single word was to disturb the impression of this extraordinary encounter. After some time the old man rose to his feet and moved to the farthest part of the apartment. When he returned, he handed Lichtenau a broad golden ring with a large oval-shaped ruby, sparkling brilliantly.

"Take it, Nabor!" he said. "Put it on the index finger of your right hand. It is a royal ring. Only an Atlantean Lucoman may wear it."

Lichtenau studied the ring with great interest. It was a piece of excellent workmanship, the huge ruby was exquisitely beautiful and there was a triangle engraved upon it. He looked up at the old sage with questioning eyes.

"The triangle is the symbol for *Elohim*'s Eye," said the old man and added, "The Atlantean Lucoman received the inner initiation in the same way as the priests of Atlantis. They were counted among the Enlightened Ones—even though not all of them were actually enlightened."

At this point the young scholar was struck abruptly by the full awareness of his position…. He tried to grasp the events in this grotto with his reasoning mind, but he could not. Was all this a dream—or was it reality? This old man was definitely a human being—and yet, there were so many mysteries surrounding him, mysteries well beyond Lichtenau's understanding. Once again, the old man seemed to have read his thoughts; he said, "Don't brood. Nabor! Your consciousness is narrow as yet—it is limited to your five senses. Only by attending the school of initiation can it be enlarged. Such initiatory schooling wakens your inner sense organs, thus enabling you to recognize and see the other Atlantean

Empires. It's not an easy path to follow; it takes time and your total devotion. You were able to see Lehuana because I lifted you out of your narrowness with my power! Now I will let you see your former life as Nabor—but I am not going to help you this time. Why? Because I want to eliminate any possibility that you might believe later that I had suggested these images to you using my will power."

"But I have no practice in conjuring up the inner vision," Lichtenau objected.

"I am going to give you something that will loosen the fetters of your earth-bound attachment, something that will lift you above all notions of time and space."

"What are you going to give me? Peyote? I'm well aware of its effectiveness, although I don't know much about what it's actually made of."

The old sage shook his head. "Its not Peyote," he said. Then he added, "Peyote is the sap of a stingless cactus. The ancient Mayas who were the descendants of Atlantean settlers originating from the kingdom of Maya—which in turn was one of twelve kingdoms of the Greater Atlantean Empire—those Mayas then, who had intermingled with the local aborigine population, passed down the knowledge about these things. In those days the people of this country used to organize great processions to bring home what they called the "flesh of god." It was carried ceremoniously into the temples and kept there for the major religious festivals. But peyote opens up the inner vision for a short time only; moreover, only limited vision will be gained through it and, if used incorrectly, it can be extremely dangerous—even deadly. What I am going to give you is sinikuiki, a potion through which thousands of years can be bridged in a moment. Sinikuiki will carry you back across long stretches in the time continuum. You will enter a bodily sheath that was yours in a previous life. You will experience pain and joy and discover connections and interrelations never before laid bare to you. You should, however, consider this: these revelations are not something you should know intellectually; rather they are something you must *live* and…ought to *live by* as well. The events of those bygone days are—as soon as you fully understand them—meant to throw light on the path of your present life."

After these words a myriad of thoughts began whizzing through Lichtenau's head. What did the old man have in mind for him? Did he plan to subject him to some sort of experiment? Was he really going to guide him back through the millennia? Was it even worth his while to participate in this project? Or was this the very moment he had imagined so often? And if he were never to wake up from this dream—what then? Lichtenau's lips twisted into a melancholy smile: Was there anyone he could think of who would miss him? "No," he thought, "there was no-one...." Finally, looking squarely at the old priest, he said, "All right, old man, give me your potion!"

The old man had remained standing in front of him during this scene and none of Lichtenau's emotions had escaped him.

"Drink this, Nabor, and have no fear! You will awaken again. All that's going to happen is that you will walk a path you have already traveled in the past." The priest poured a few drops of the liquid into the agate cup before him. Watching with interest, Lichtenau said, "Will you stay with me, old friend?"

"I will stay near you and give you an energy shield, so to speak. No being of darkness will be able to approach you. So have no fear! Just concentrate on the name *Nabor*—and you will become Nabor."

The old man made a gesture of blessing over Lichtenau who, once again, was engulfed by supernatural silence.... He sat motionless for a while and, feeling the silence around him like a protective shield, he picked up the cup and drank. Gradually all heaviness slipped from him.... It seemed to him that he was floating—then, a sudden but gentle jolt—and he began to glide off into higher states. The walls of the apartment dissolved into bright light.

Large, open windows, framed by curvilinear columns, offered a view onto a vast inner court embellished by marble arcades shimmering in the blazing sunlight. One of the doorway curtains opened and a tall man clad in a long red silk robe entered. He put his right hand to his heart and bowed deeply.

"Who are you?"

A flash of surprise passed over the man's face, then he said: "Ekloh, your Chamberlain, Sire."

Nabor moved his hand slightly across his forehead, "I was dreaming, Ekloh."

"Mamya, the Palace Steward, is waiting in the Hall, Sire. He will accompany you to the Temple. The Lucoman Maya is waiting for you there."

Nabor rose and looked down at himself. Somehow he felt like a stranger in this festive dress. Suddenly he realized that his ring was missing. He glanced round searchingly....

"What are you looking for, Sire?" the Chamberlain asked.

"The ring with the ruby. I had it...."

Ekloh looked at his master with a smile. "You are still confused by your dream, Sire. The royal ring will be adorning your hand only after having become the Lucoman's husband."

Nabor nodded, his gaze still vague, as if in a dream. Passing his right hand over his eyes, he stood up straight and tall and shook his blond hair from his forehead. He made a sign with his hand and the Chamberlain left. Again the curtain was pushed aside and Mamya, the Steward of the Palace, stood before him.

"Hail, Nabor, son of Ebor, the Great Lucoman of the Raya Kingdom! Milady, the Lucoman of Maya, sends her solemn greetings. She is awaiting you in *Elohim*'s Temple to become one with you before His Face."

Mamya made a deep bow and continued, "According to ancient custom, there will be six sons of kings accompanying you to the Temple."

Nabor left the apartment with measured steps. The princes awaiting him in the Hall cheered as he emerged. As he saw them there and felt their genuine joy, his relaxed bearing returned to him. He shook hands with each one warmly. Then Arel of Baya stepped forward and made a somewhat sarcastic little speech. He spoke with mock ceremony as he said:

"Great and powerful Sire, Master of the beautiful Maya and her Kingdom! Our heads are bowed in respect—but also in distress, for you are obviously willing to forsake our—your friends'—affection for a woman's love. Oh—but you must not think that we are angry with you; you should know however, O Audacious One, that you have chosen to follow a dangerous path; it is easier indeed to tame a wild horse than the whimsical heart of a beautiful woman!"

Nabor burst out laughing. "Don't you worry, companion of my youth! Ebor's son will always hold the same loyalty to all of you that you have for him." Then he added in a lower voice and as if embarrassed,

"Maya, too, whose proud heart has chosen me will honor you as my friends."

The banter between them continued as Nabor tried to defend his action as best he could, when the Steward finally came to his rescue.

"It is time, Sire. The watchmen on the Towers tell us that the sun has reached its highest position. All the ruling kings of Eya-Eya have assembled in the Temple." These last words were accompanied by the sound of bugles from outside.

Nabor, his expression serious once more, nodded. A sudden foreboding told him that the power and splendor awaiting him would put an end to the lighthearted and carefree days of his youth. How delightful his life had been in the royal palace of Rayagard, romping about with his brother and his friends. How wonderful it had been learning to ride the most spirited horses, to race his team-of-four in the Arena while the crowd was cheering. Gone forever were the days he, his beloved mother Lehuana's favorite child, had spent sitting at her feet in the royal barque as they were rowed down the canals that branched out everywhere into the beautiful countryside. What a marvelous homeland he had! All those orange groves, those chestnut gardens, those dark green olive fields interspersed with so many flowering meadows! And then all the animals grazing peacefully and moving about at their leisure, everywhere! And now—suddenly—he was to become King beside the most beautiful woman ever to occupy one of the thrones of Eya-Eya: Maya, the heiress to the Mayan Kingdom. He had often seen her, accompanied by her father, the old Lucoman Petyn.

His own father and Petyn had been good friends. They had always stuck together, had borne their joys and their pains together. He recalled how upset his father had been the day his best friend's son was hurled to the ground during a chariot race and had died of his wounds. Old king Petyn's heart was broken by his untimely death and he had been unable to recover from that fateful blow. But he had also been tormented by thoughts about the future of his kingdom. Of course, there was his daughter, a magnificent creature at the height of her beauty who had helped her broken father with her unusual capacities for reason and vigor—but he had never forgotten that neither the Loki (the king of all the priests of the Empire) nor other kings would agree to the reign of a woman in the Mayan Kingdom. For this reason, he had asked his friend Ebor if Nabor, Ebor's second son, would marry his daughter. And so—despite all the warnings spoken by Lehuana, who had considered the match between her favorite child and the strong-willed daughter of the Mayan Lucoman a dangerous undertaking, he had obtained Ebor's consent. From his deathbed, Petyn had asked his daughter to pledge that she would accept Nabor as her husband and transfer all ruling power to him. Although Maya had given her word, within and in secret her pride rebelled; she wanted to be the only ruler of the kingdom. To encourage the other kings to look favorably upon her plan, she had dispatched envoys to them with precious gifts but everywhere she had met with nothing but polite—indeed astonished—refusal. Since the early days of the first twelve kings, only men had run the course of events in Eya-Eya. The thought of a young female claiming the throne of the Mayan Kingdom—on the grounds of royal descent—had seemed to them both ridiculous and unacceptable. However, the proud Maya did not give up so easily. She engaged a priest who was devoted to her to intervene in her favor with the Loki. Unfortunately, the Priest-King's reply was brief and to the point, and not unlike an order:

"You pledged your word to a dying man and you will keep your promise and accept Nabor, Ebor's son, as Lucoman of the Mayan Kingdom. Should you try to break your holy vow, Nabor will become the ruler of the country without marrying you and you will be detailed to the amazons' regiment. This is my decision. You had better do as you are told—or the days of your splendor are over."

Another person would have been shattered by the almighty Loki's answer but in Maya's case it only stiffened her resistance. Uninvited, she had appeared with her resplendent entourage at the annual meeting between the Lucoman and the King of Priests at Bayagard, the capital of the Baya Kingdom. She intended to participate in this convention (which always took place in the Great Temple at the time of the equinox, a meeting at which the Loki gave the kings their general directions for political action in the coming year) as the fully authorized representative of her kingdom. But the Loki had refused to admit her. He met her with icy coldness and, again, insisted that she keep her promise. Maya had raced back to Mayagard in hot fury. She had no wish to give in and it was only the many serious remonstrations on the part of her experienced ministers that had finally convinced her to send Ebor a flattering message, declaring that she was ready to enter into wedlock with his son Nabor.

And now their wedding-day had arrived.

Nabor had traveled to Mayagard with his parents and with all the grandees of Eya-Eya, who had joined them along with their spouses and entourage. Only the Loki was not present. He never left his Temple-Fortress at Bayagard and had sent the High Priest Tenupo to unite the two royal children and to transmit his blessings to them. All guests rejoiced at the disobedient princess' change of heart, a change which prevented any irrevocable measure of punishment that might otherwise have been taken against her. Hence this wedding day was a day of joy for everyone.

These were the thoughts that Nabor was turning over in his mind. Again he recalled his worried mother saying, "Stay as you are, my son! Discipline yourself and stay clean! Avoid wine and try to be a good friend to your wife!"

All his friends waiting in the vast Hall had fallen silent; everyone's eyes were on Nabor; finally, Arel of Baya cried out, "He's day-dreaming again, our great Nabor!" and brought his hand down heavily on Nabor's shoulder. Nabor looked around suddenly, as if unsure of where he was. Loud laughter erupted on all sides as he pulled himself together, signed to Mamya and, followed by the crowd, left the Hall.

Carriages with teams-of-four were waiting in front of the broad steps leading up to the entrance of the Palace. The muscular arms of the charioteers were barely able to keep the impatient horses in check. As Nabor stepped into the open, the crowd's cheers surged up toward him like a tidal wave. The sun—now at its zenith—immersed the beautiful scene before his eyes in a golden brilliance, its rays broken only by the large inlays of turquoise and sapphire in the outer walls of the marble palaces, stones which sent refracted bundles of light in all directions. Trumpets sounded from the tops of the palace towers, their peals intermingling with the fine chimes of the aeolian harps and resounding like from the rooftops like the Music of the Spheres. The wide, palm-lined streets were covered with a carpet of flowers and a shower of the most beautiful blossoms descended on the procession from above. Nabor was happier now, as his youthfulness finally got the better of him. He began to wave to all sides and caught flowers in mid-air before throwing them back into the crowd—which triggered renewed cheers.

The cavalcade stopped in front of the Temple, a massive circular structure of white marble with four slender towers rising from the top of the walls at each of the cardinal points. Larger-than-life statues of the twelve royal couples encircled the temple. With its roof made from plates of beaten gold and its bejeweled walls, the Temple stood apart, scintillating in the blazing sunlight. The large gates to the inner courtyard were ajar. Priests and priestesses dressed in long silk robes stood on both sides of the large flight of stairs leading up to the gates. All of them wore a golden headband with a four-pointed star—the symbol of Light—in its center. Ornate scarves flowed down in intricate folds from their heads to their shoulders, held in place by the headbands.

Still standing on the steps, Nabor considered the homage offered to him by the crowd, then he swiftly stepped into the inner court where he was greeted by another festive assembly. All the Lucoman were there, dressed in variegated, gem-studded robes. Many of the ladies wore gowns of a transparent, veil-like material interlaced with silver threads which accented the harmonious beauty of their bodies. With precious jewelry on their heads, hands and arms—and many a slim ankle set off by a pretty golden anklet—the ladies stood sparkling in their luxuriant ornaments!

The Lucoman's many attendants were also there: Palace Managers, Chamberlains and their richly decked out ladies. Boys and girls dressed in white frocks with flower wreaths in their hair were ready to begin chanting the age-old hymns praising *Elohim*. Behind them were the flutists and oboists, the harpists, percussionists, and pipers. Against one of the walls stood an organ-like instrument with just a few large golden pipes but which gave the Atlantean music its unmistakable sound. Nabor went up to his parents. Ebor, the old Lucoman, was deeply moved as he took his son into his arms; his mother breathed a kiss upon her darling's forehead. Nabor paid appropriate respect to the rest of the Lucoman by putting his right hand across his heart and bowing to them.

The heavy curtains which isolated the innermost sanctum of the Temple drew back. The intoxicating fragrance of frankincense pervaded the air. Young priests formed a row on each side of the aisle and festive music began playing as Nabor and the other young princes stepped into the inner chamber of the Temple. This was a high and spacious room divided into two by a curtain running down its center. One's feet sank into soft carpets covering the marble floor. Dim light streamed in from above. Only the priests' white robes seemed to shine brightly in the mystical twilight. Wood fires were smoldering in pans sat upon golden tripods on both sides of the room—fires which flared up from time to time whenever a priest's hand threw incense into them. Unsure and somewhat anxious, Nabor stopped as his companions positioned themselves around him. Then the curtain in the center of the room moved and an old priest entered the room. He raised both hands in a blessing gesture of welcome and said in a deep voice, "*Elohim* bless your coming to this Temple, Nabor!" As he came closer, Nabor recognized him as the High Priest Tenupo, the Loki's own representative. Respectfully, he bowed to the worthy elder whose face was framed by a white beard and whose kind eyes were looking at him with encouragement. Tenupo raised his hands once again before letting them glide down alongside Nabor's body who at once felt as if enveloped by a warm flow of power—a power that seemed to carry and support him. Tenupo repeated this ritual three times mumbling as he did so through lips which barely moved at all:

"May thee be filled with *Elohim*'s Light! May the God's Light envelope thee!"

All the while subordinate priests continued to stir the wood fires burning in their trivets and dense clouds of frankincense fragrance rose up into the air; the ambrosial perfume almost took Nabor's breath away. The old priest finally stepped away from him. On cue, the subordinates closed the curtain to the inner court.

"Put the royal cloak around his shoulders!" Tenupo ordered the royal princes—and two subordinate priests handed them a wide, sky-blue mantle with edges embroidered with rubies which flared up like red fires. Then two of the princes laid the cloak around Nabor's shoulders.

"Bend your head, Nabor, and receive the royal jewels!" Tenupo bid him—whereupon two other princes wrapped the thrice-folded royal scarf around Nabor's head, fixing it in place with a mosaic-like ribbon embroidered with rubies and turquoise.

The highest symbol of the Lucoman, the royal ring, was brought forth on a golden platter and handed to Tenupo. It was a large, heavy golden ring with a ruby the size of a bird's egg. Holding this jewel in his left hand, the old priest came up to Nabor. A sudden solemn silence overtook the premises, even the music had stopped. All present held their breath, the great moment had come—Nabor was to be raised to the rank of Lucoman. Tenupo's voice filled the room when he said, "Nabor, *Elohim* gives Maya, Petyn's daughter, in your hand. He raises you to be the ruler of the Mayas and will count you from now on among His highest servants. Promise in your heart to respect His Commandments as proof you are worthy of His great Mercy!"

"I promise," was Nabor's barely audible response.

"Give me your hand then!" Tenupo's thin hand seized Nabor's right hand with a firm grasp. His eyes were sparkling with joy behind his penetrating gaze. Minutes passed as a breathless silence hung in the Hall, the young Lucoman calmly enduring the scrutinizing stare of the older priest. Finally, Tenupo pulled Nabor closer and kissed him on the head before putting the royal ring on the index finger of his right hand.

"Your heart is pure, Nabor. Your pledge was heard and is accepted. Always go your way in accordance with *Elohim*'s commandments; He will enlighten you and you will see His Light—and the triangle on your ring will become an inner truth."

Nabor was overwhelmed and had difficulty in keeping his composure. No wonder: So many things had assailed him in the course of the last few days, thoroughly remodeling his entire life.

In the inner court, the marvelous chanting of the choir had begun. Soon trumpets and stringed instruments joined in. Tenupo's glance once more enveloped the young ruler—he could sense Nabor's emotion and decided to draw him to him and assist him in carrying out his high office. Then he turned to the central curtain—whereupon it was immediately pulled open by subordinate priests—and there before them stood Maya. She was dressed in the same royal cloak as Nabor and surrounded by royal princesses and priestesses. She stood there in proud beauty, her auburn hair arranged in a braided crown with a single pearl fixed in its center. Her large green opalescent eyes were reminiscent of the vastness and the colors of the sea. Nabor stood lost in this wonderful sight. To him, Maya looked like a goddess. As their eyes met, she could not help but sense the deep admiration he held for her. As he made a step toward her, any remaining remnants of her hard exterior dissolved. She had entered the Temple with an inner reluctance and had endured all the ceremonies in silence. To her, it had seemed that this day was to put the final seal of authentication on her defeat. With her pride wounded to the quick, she had to force herself to smile. In all those eyes upon her she had felt nothing but scorn. Time and again in her apartments, her adviser and Palace Steward Mamya had tried to soothe her emotions when she had released her bitterness in free-flowing outbursts.

"Nabor is a dreamer, Milady," he had told her. "It will be easy for you to make him comply with your wishes. You will continue to rule and the handsome boy will be grateful to you for taking the burden of government off his shoulders. He has not, so far, known a woman physically. You will be the first one. He will adore you. Be wise, Milady, and use your beauty well!"

And now that same Nabor was standing before her in all his regal splendor! His face expressed joyful excitement and his eyes spoke a clear and unmistakable language: they enveloped her with a flood of admiration and loving warmth. She was struck by his beauty. "I think, I could love him!"

Both of them remained lost in each others sight for some time. Then Tenupo came up to them, took their hands and put them together, disclosing the last secret to them:

"Thus, reunited once again, you who have already spent one long life-time together, united in love and fidelity for the benefit of many. Keep this holy moment in your hearts forever, this instant when by *Elohim*'s Mercy you were given to each other once more. Efface the "I" in your hearts, live with the "Thou," then the radiance of His Light will forever shine upon your road. May *Elohim* bless you wherever you go!"

Nabor's innocent heart absorbed the old priests words willingly. Maya herself could not avoid their impact and a soft smile illuminated her proud and beautiful face, making it blossom with warm emotion. Nabor noticed the change with joy.

"Maya," he stammered. "Maya, my wife."

He drew her to him and for the first time their lips touched. Tenupo held his hands high above their heads and blessed them, great kindness shining on his face.

A wave of pulsating heat vibrated through Maya's features. She looked up in her embarrassment but in that moment she felt her husband's hand in hers and quickly recovered her self-assurance. The curtain between them and the inner court opened. Preceded by the other royal sons and daughters and followed by Tenupo, the priests and the priestesses, the pair left the inner precincts of the Temple. In the courtyard they received the good wishes and blessings of their parents, the nobility of Atlantis and other guests.

They were bathed in the sounds of jubilant music interwoven to exquisite harmony with the choir's voices as they stepped out through the gates of the Temple. There they stood in the blinding brilliance of the Atlantean sun as the thunderous cheers of the waiting crowd mixed with the sound of the bugles. Nabor and Maya slowly descended the long flight of stairs to the square in front of the Temple, where Nabor turned round and looked back. Old Tenupo stood at the wide open gates of the Temple, his arms raised in a gesture of blessing. Nabor let go of Maya's hand to return the greeting. A brief moment of annoyance seemed to rise in the Lucoman' heart—she was not fond of priests and had set up inner defenses against their influence, but the special nature of this moment overrode her emotions.

Preceded by children strewing flowers and surrounded by the flamboyant joy of the people, the royal couple—proud, straight and in slender tallness—proceeded through the streets to the Palace, where the great royal wedding meal was going to be served.

The young couple was surrounded by festive events for several days and had little opportunity to come closer to each other. For Nabor these days passed like a dream of unearthly beauty. Maya was also happy and seemed perfectly relaxed. Her husband hardly ever left her side, always endeavoring to make her the center of attention, while he, himself, remained in the background.

When she saw her darling son's happiness, Lehuana's misgivings also melted away and the old queen was able to offer a more affectionate farewell to Maya than she had previously thought possible.

The sun was blazing down upon the golden roofs of Mayagard, making them glow like miniature suns. Outside of town the ocean's waves were lapping against the shore and from the beaches to the Temple lay an almost endless expanse of flowers, blooming shrubs and trees, endowing the countryside with the magnificence of a paradise. Magnolia trees shed their flowers, covering the grassy surfaces below them with thick layers of balmy petals. Maya, the young Lucoman strolled lightly across these "carpets." Her feet moved carefully as she passed, as if dancing rather than walking. Happiness shone from her eyes. "Now I don't have to strut about ceremoniously any more," she thought and smiled. "Nabor will have to do that! The burden has been shifted to *his* shoulders now." Her eyes darkened. Suddenly, a small monkey jumped across her path, barely avoiding her feet. The little animal stopped and threw a nut at her. She bent down toward the monkey and as she sank her gaze into those shrewd little eyes, the tiny creature leapt aside with a shriek.

Maya continued ambling along toward the ocean. The cliffs plunged down steeply at the spot she had chosen and waves were bouncing over the jutting rocks below. Suddenly Maya stopped. There was a man sitting on the large rock out there in the sea. No doubt about it, it was Nabor. "Strange," she said to herself, "Nabor all by himself sitting on a rock…!" The sun's rays were dancing around him and, when he saw her, he began waving his hand at her joyfully. He climbed into a small boat and signaled to her to move further down along the coast to where one of the many canals that had been built by the Atlantean master-architects ran into the sea. There she awaited him as he came up to her rowing with powerful thrusts. He was dressed in a white garment and she saw the muscles of his arms working under his bracelets.

"Why did you not take one of the boys with you?" she called out to him.

"What would I have done with a boy?" he replied. "He would only have disturbed me." His boat had come up to her, he stopped, and she jumped aboard. She landed right in his arms and he gave her a big hug.

"Is my Queen happy?" he asked, holding her.

"She is, Nabor."

He continued rowing along the canal which led to the water-gate of Asgard. They disappeared through the gate behind which they were met by palace boys who were waiting there to attend to them. They entered the Lucoman's apartment walking hand in hand like two little children. Maya moved to a small table upon which stood an alabaster cup. Out of this she took a small object carved in wood. She showed it to Nabor and asked, "What do you think this might be? I found it on the beach a few days ago. It was probably washed in by the sea."

Nabor studied the object, turning it over in his hands, and said,

"It seems to be the wooden effigy of a deity as primitive peoples use them. Throw it away, Maya! Foreign gods will bring no luck!"

Maya took back the figurine and looked at it with interest. "I don't think it's a god, Nabor. It's only an image of sorts. Perhaps the one it belongs to will soon come to retrieve it." With these words she carried the little statue to a golden chest lined with red silk and cautiously placed it in one of the corners. Nabor watched her and shook his head, but he had no time to comment further, as the curtain was parted that very moment by two palace boys carrying dishes filled with various fruits. Maya clapped her hands. "Come on, Nabor, this will do us good after this morning's outing!"

And they sat together like two children, snatching things from each other in fun only to offer them back again later. Again the curtain was parted and a tall blond boy walked into the room. Nabor looked up.

"Mamya, the Palace Steward, is asking for permission to appear before you, Sire," the boy said.

The Lucoman's face grew serious. What might Mamya want at this hour, he wondered. He turned to Maya.

"Let him come, Nabor! We'll hear what news he has to tell us," she said.

Nabor nodded in consent and Mamya entered. He bowed before the young couple. Nabor was not very fond of the man; he considered him somewhat too slick, too careful and canny with his words. The Steward was well aware of the Lucoman's cool reserve and tried to gain his favor through measured doses of friendliness. In a somewhat harsh tone, Nabor asked him,

"What brings you here, Mamya?"

"Something terrible has happened, Sire. Kaana, the Lucoman of the Waya Empire, has slain his brother while in a state of drunkenness," came his distraught answer.

Maya jumped to her feet with a cry. A human being murdered! This was something unheard of! Never before had anything as monstrous as this happened in Eya-Eya. Nabor stood up, also in a state of intense agitation. He had turned pale and exclaimed, "I cannot believe you Mamya! This must be a mean joke you're playing on us."

"One of your father's messengers is outside; he will bear testimony to the truth of my words, Sire."

"Fetch him, I want to see him," Nabor bellowed.

After a few moments Mamya returned with the messenger—an elderly man with unusually calm movements and quiet eyes. He waited humbly for the Lucoman to address him.

"Let us hear my father's message!" Nabor ordered.

The messenger's voice began to ring out, as if trained to soothe the prevailing fluster of minds. He said,

"The Lucoman Ebor sends you his fatherly salutations and blessings!"

Hearing his father's name mentioned, the young ruler instinctively bowed down. The messenger continued, "Overpowered by the sinister demons of the Realm of Darkness and while in a state of drunken intoxication, Kaana, the Lucoman of the Wayas, has slain in wrathful anger the youth Ebale, his brother. Never before was such great a crime committed in any of the harmonious kingdoms of Eya-Eya—a nation where human beings and animals enjoy their life in the peace of *Elohim*'s Grace. Take up your arms, my son, and go to Bayagard! The Loki, the great Huatami, has called together the Kings of Atlantis to gather in a Great Royal Council to be held in the Temple during the Holy Night of Light. Greetings to your wife!"

Having spoken thus, the messenger fell silent. Nabor stood there, utterly confounded by what he had just heard. Deep inside himself he sensed that this terrible deed must bring great misery to the country, as the life of a brother was holy to the Atlanteans who—to every extent possible—even protected animals from being killed. Hence the fearlessness and the peaceful coexistence of panther and ox throughout the country. And now, suddenly, blood had been shed, the most precious blood of all: human blood. Nabor clasped his head with both hands—he still could not believe it. Maya sat on the couch, pale and with a disconcerted look in her eyes. She too was deeply aware of the outrage this felony would bring. Shudders ran down her spine and her lips trembled. She kept her eyes on Nabor, now walking the floor in a state of great agitation.

"I wonder what the Loki will do in a situation like this" Maya heard him say to himself. At this the Lucoman's face regained its color, her eyes darkened and an expression of disdain appeared around her mouth. She said coldly,

"I wonder, will Huatami's power be great enough to bring the murdered man back to life?"

Nabor stopped at once and looked at his wife in dismay

"What are you talking about, Maya!" Staring at her, he suddenly realized that he was looking at the face of stranger. Was this his Maya, the soft, affectionate woman he loved so much? It was as if icy fingers had touched his heart. At once he knew that he had nothing at all in common with this disdainful woman, one whose tone of voice could hold so much contempt. It was as if a frosty mood had permeated the room. Mamya said quickly,

"In accordance with his high office, the Loki will transmit to the Council of the Lucoman *Elohim*'s decision."

At this Maya curled her lips in mockery, but said nothing. Nabor had walked to the window and was searching the wide blue expanse of the sky with his eyes. The transformation he had just witnessed in Maya had wounded him to the depths of his being. He had been brought up by devoted parents who had instilled the awe of *Elohim* in him and His mediator, the Priest-king, who had always appeared to him like a demigod. Maya's utterances had thrown him into an inner conflict between religious faith and love. No doubt, the Loki was also a human being but didn't he live *like a true recluse* in his Temple-Fortress in Bayagard?

The Lucoman saw him only once a year when he came out to hold council with them and to announce—while in a state of trance—the Commandments of the God of Light. In the royal palace of Bayagard the Loki was spoken of only in a subdued voice and with great respect. At their last meeting, Nabor's father, who was widely respected and loved for his sense of justice, had said, "Preserve your faith in the Loki! He knows more than we do; he is the guardian of Eya-Eya's happiness. Nobody else can take his place for he is enlightened by *Elohim*'s Light." As Nabor remembered these words, he suddenly thought: "Maya is young!" He knew of Maya's struggle for recognition, of her claim to reign and government; he was well aware of how much her pride had suffered. And yet, even now there seemed some bitter feelings stirring within her heart. Hadn't his love made her happy?

"I am going to help her," he said to himself, brooding. "I am going to do all I can to fill her life with light and love."

Inner turmoil showed on his young manly face. He turned around, stepped up to his wife and sat down beside her. He spoke kindly when he said, "Don't think about it, Maya! It is not for us to say what Huatami's task is or is not."

At these words Maya's features lost their rigidity and a smile began to blossom across her face. Almost imperceptibly, she nestled against her husband. Nabor turned to Mamya. "Mamya," he said, "have a royal lodging prepared as befits my father's messenger." Uttering words of thanks, the latter withdrew along with the Steward.

"My love!" Nabor embraced his beautiful wife and with his right hand gently stroking the luxurious hair piled atop her head, his lips breathed tender kisses upon her eyes and searched for her mouth. Maya was contented as she allowed herself to be enveloped in waves of tenderness. Her finely sculptured hands also began to caress Nabor, her sensuous mouth yielded to her husband's wooing: The two young hearts were beating together.... The first instance of disharmony in their marriage was all but forgotten.

Eventually, the day of Nabor's departure arrived as palace officials and chamberlains awaited the Lucoman in the Great Hall.

"The King is in the Queen's apartments," Ekloh whispered to Mamya and a fine smile crossed Mamya's lips: Maya was probably giving last-minute instructions to her husband. But Mamya was mistaken. Maya was only helping her friend and husband ready himself for his journey. She had taken care of all the practical details—down to the smallest of necessities, and Nabor was touched by so much thoughtfulness.

"I'll soon be with you again, my love," he said tenderly. "I can't stand being apart from you for long."

Happily, Maya cuddled up against him; he was all hers and nobody could take him away from her. Hand in hand they entered the Great Hall.

"Mamya, Premenio, and Xernio shall accompany me!" the Lucoman commanded and the three men joined their master. Then the royal couple walked slowly through the Palace's gates and onto the broad steps outside. Nabor embraced his wife once more before climbing into his chariot. The other officials, Ekloh the Chamberlain, and a large number of stewards and servants filled the other vehicles, while a cavalry troop swarmed around them.

Nabor took the reins and the whip from the charioteer's hands and let the whip smack above the horses' heads. The team-of-four leaped into motion at once, almost causing the light-weight carriage to rise into the air. Nabor saluted Maya with a laugh as he passed by and the entire party set off on their journey, stirring up a great cloud of dust in their wake.

Sprawling for many miles along the southern coastline of the island, Bayagard was the oldest and largest urban settlement of the country. The city was connected to the sea and other Atlantean towns by a network of canals. Even within the city itself there were—besides the roads and ordinary streets—canals running in every direction. All the wealth and riches produced in Eya-Eya could be found in Bayagard: the flat roofs were covered with sheets of gold, the walls of the buildings encrusted with semiprecious stones. The only building material used was marble and in all possible shades and colors. As if stretching toward the heavens, the battlements of the palaces were topped by towers upon which harps had been installed, each serving the wind as a musical instrument. Hence the air was constantly filled with melodious humming and ringing. The canals were teeming with barges and boats of all sizes. Now and again a larger vessel, propelled by an army of rowers and belonging to some person in high office or a position of power, could be seen passing by. Luxuriant vegetation lined the streets, the squares and filled the gardens of private houses and palaces, filling the air with an almost intoxicating perfume. The Loki's Temple-Fortress, a city in itself, rose from a hill and was surrounded by a wide circular canal. Girdled by mighty walls, this Fortress sheltered the Great Temple, the Loki's personal villa and the dwellings of priests and attendants. Although this Temple resembled those in other capital cities, it surpassed them all in its majestic lay-out and paraphernalia.

As this was the day of the summer solstice, all Bayagard was in a feverish excitement. The Holy Feast of Light would be turning this particular night into day. All royal rulers in the Empire had arrived in the city for the occasion. The Palace of the Lucoman of Bayagard was vast enough to accommodate all the high-ranking guests and their entourage.

The citizens were busy making preparations for the Night of Light by stacking huge piles of fragrant wood upon the roofs and the broad upper top of the city-wall. All barges and boats were decorated with garlands of flowers and the streets through which the procession of kings would make its way from the Palace of the Lucoman to the Fortress of the Great Temple were richly festooned with floral decorations. The sun was shining brightly. All the roads leading to Bayagard were filled with crowds of people approaching by foot or carriage to take part in the celebration. The stream of visitors flowing toward the city was like an unending human river.

But there was also a curious group of individuals that attracted attention: Surrounded by horsemen, an elderly man leaning on a walking stick was moving through the dust of the road. His face was deadly pale. With his eyes deep in their sockets, his disheveled hair and beard hanging down from his deeply bent head, he seemed to be pressed down by some invisible burden. The man wore only a rough cloth in the color of the earth. It was Kaana, the assassin of his brother, Ebale. This man, who had been the ruler of the Waya Kingdom, had plummeted from the highest position of power and most sublime splendor into the deepest disgrace imaginable. Lower than the lowest servant, despised and shunned by all, as an outlaw he now walked the long and painful road to the city of the Priest-King to hear his sentence. His people had cast him off, had turned away from him who had soiled his hands with the blood of a human being. Behind him walked a slender woman whose features were numbed by deep woe and whose eyes seemed to be gazing into a dimension of non-being. A young man supported her. The Lucoman Hethara—it was she—uttered a groan. The torments of the last few days had worn her down, her feet hurt with every step. At the sight of his mother's wretchedness her son's heart contracted painfully. He wanted to carry her but she refused. She dragged herself further with her remaining willpower.

Suddenly shouts were heard; horsemen were approaching at great speed and behind them a cloud of dust came rolling in. The riders shouted, "Give way for the Lucoman!" before the magnificent train of carriages came rattling along. On the first of the chariots, Nabor could be seen standing beside the charioteer.

The wretched little party had apparently attracted his interest also. Did he see correctly? Was that not Cerbio, the cheerful Cerbio who had accompanied him to the Temple the day of his wedding to Maya? He ordered his charioteer to halt the vehicle.

"Cerbio, my friend!" Nabor jumped down from his chariot and went up to his friend. A glimmer of joy passed over Cerbio's face which, however, turned serious again almost at once. Stepping back, he exclaimed,

"Don't touch me, Nabor! Bad guilt separates us from all those whose hands are clean."

Nabor stood as if dazed, his heart filled with compassion. He said, "You are free from guilt—and so is your mother. I shall help you. Come to me in my Kingdom and I will make you forget your predicament!" He held out his hand.

"Your intention honors you, Nabor, but we will never leave our father in this moment of deepest misery," Cerbio replied—adding in a low voice, "...unless blood is returned for blood."

A deep groan escaped the Lucoman's lips—a sound which, in its bitterness, went straight to Nabor's heart. Shaken by the sight of such inexpressible human suffering, he bowed down to the royal lady in deep respect, before his gaze returned to Cerbio, the friend from his youth. A silent exchange of farewells between the two friends—and Nabor mounted his carriage. This encounter with human misery had left him with a sinister impression that had darkened his day. He paid no attention to the golden battlements of Bayagard glittering in the distance. Later, as the shadows of the night lowered themselves toward the Earth, crowds began gathering in the festive streets. Shortly before midnight, a long procession of Temple attendants appeared—boys in short white frocks and with a wreath of flowers in their hair. Carrying wooden torches drenched in oil, they took up position on both sides of the road. Soon the crowd fell silent, the only sound still to be heard was the delicate humming of the wind-harps. All eyes were turned in expectation to the dark, massive outline of the Temple-Fortress.

Suddenly fires flared up upon the towers of the Temple and trumpets were blown, their long drawn-out sounds picked up by the sentinels on the towers atop other palaces and sent on from there to still further palace roofs. By now, fires were flaring up everywhere. A group of priests—clearly directing their measured steps to the Lucoman's Palace—was seen crossing the bridge between the Temple-Fortress and the city. Upon reaching its gates, one of the priests knocked on the door and the Lucoman of Bayagard stepped out almost at once. The priest said, "The Loki sends his blessings. He will make known to you what *Elohim* has revealed to him."

The Lucoman bowed deeply and replied, "Our hearts are open to receive the divine message."

The priest turned around and motioned to the temple boys nearest to him to light their torches. Quickly all the other boys followed suit and soon a chain of burning fires was running right up to the Temple-Fortress.

Led on by the priests and deferentially greeted by the crowd, the Lucoman's cavalcade began moving through the streets. Behind each of them were stewards carrying the long train of the royal coat. Nabor, the youngest of the Lucoman, was the last in line. The festivity of the occasion—harmoniously in tune with the brilliant resplendence of the lights burning everywhere, the fragrance of the flowers and the solemn melodies ringing out from the flutes as well as the jingles of the bells carried ahead of the procession—all this, together with the splendor of the starstrewn nightly sky, made the young man temporarily forget his earlier sorrowful thoughts. But soon enough, he was reminded of them again because the moment the royal procession was approaching the bridge, there, not far away, in the light of the torches, stood Kaana with his family.

Nabor recognized them as he drew closer. His eyes began to search for Cerbio but he had bent his head and was gazing to the ground. Nabor's heart grew heavy with sadness; all his happiness left him: once more his entire mind was focused on his friend's fate. Not even the grand reception given the Lucoman by the High Priest Tenupo on the square in front of the Temple, nor the chanting of the priests and the Temple choir —indeed the entire overwhelming magnificence of the occasion—none of this was powerful enough to drag him from his gloom. But eventually he too, led by two priests, entered the Hall of Kings of the Temple. This room, entirely laid out in white marble and domed by a high ceiling which offered a view of the night sky through a large aperture in its center, was supported by twelve mighty columns of yellow marble upon which had been affixed the emblems of the twelve kingdoms of Eya-Eya: Aya, Baya, Daya, Faya, Gaya, Kaya, Laya, Maya, Paya, Raya, Taya and Waya.

Each of the Lucoman went to stand by the column marked with the symbol of his kingdom respectively. Nabor was led to his kingdom's column by two priests and took up his position there. Only the column of the Waya Kingdom remained unoccupied. While all the Lucoman stood in silence, solemn chanting was to be heard in the great court outside of the Hall of Kings: Today the sons of the Earth were calling on the Beings of Light in *Elohim*'s Realm. They did so by means of alternating incantations of the priests' choir on the one hand, and a single boy's bell-like voice on the other, before all the boys' voices rang out at once in one overwhelming jubilation. And when the flutes and trumpets finally set in as well, music filled the entire Temple, ringing out into the still night air.

Then, as the chanting came to an end, melting away in gentle, joyful rhythms, the heavy curtain separating the Holy chamber from the Hall of Kings opened—and there he was, sitting on a throne-like seat and illumined by oil-drenched torches: the Priest-King Huatami. He was wrapped in a white garment and from his shoulders flowed a heavy white silk coat. His was the face of an ascetic and his eyes shone with unearthly brilliance. Having fasted for three days and nights, the Loki was now in a state of total absorption in the Deity. A glow of Light was streaming from him—a glow melting into the light emitted by the torches and surrounding his entire body like an aura. A murmur of awe greeted his appearance from those who had been awaiting him on the square.

Huatami rose to his feet and came forward in measured steps. He entered the Hall of Kings and the Lucoman bowed to him by lifting their hands to their foreheads, palms turned outward. The Loki went to the very center of the Hall from where he gave a blessing to all the rulers of Eya-Eya, turning to each one of them individually. Then the curtain between the Temple's inner court and the Holy chamber was closed again: Huatami and the rulers of Atlantis were alone.

Nabor shot furtive glances at the powerful Priest-King: for seconds their eyes locked. To Nabor it was as if a bolt of lightning had cut through him; he closed his eyes. Then Huatami appealed to the Deity. He first gave his thanks to *Elohim* for His protection and prayed for the enlightenment of the Lucoman of Eya-Eya and for himself—whereupon he fell silent, his gaze fixed and unseeing. He stood motionless like a statue and it was as if the silence within the Hall of Kings was suddenly filled with unseen phenomena. The Lucoman held their breath when Huatami's insisting voice announced softly and as if coming from afar, "In this holy hour Heaven and Earth unite! Listen, O Thee Kings of Atlantis, what *Elohim*, the mighty God of Light, has revealed to you: Blood was shed; a demented man slew his brother. Never before was such a dreadful deed committed in any of the Kingdoms of Eya-Eya. *Elohim* does not want us to return like for like, for the power of retribution is His. However, the assassin whose hands are soiled with blood must no longer remain within the Atlantean community. By his deed he shut himself out of our circle. In my quality as First Servant to the Great Spirit, I herewith announce *Elohim*'s sentence: For destroying a human shroud of the Eternal Spirit Kaana be cursed! Repudiated by our people as he is now, may he find his food among the animals of the fields! May his foot be unsafe and may he be on the run from this day hence! Driven by the burden of his guilt, may he spend the days of his misery in solitude! No-one is to give him shelter, all are to shun him! Exiled to the barren Northern Mountains, may he spend his guilty life no better than a beast!"

Huatami fell silent. The kings stood by their columns gazing gloomily to the ground. Everybody was aware of the terrible nature of this verdict, yet in the face of the outrageous crime committed by Kaana, nobody's heart was moved to compassion. The Loki continued in a softer voice, "However, the wife of the guilty man shall be free. The evil deed severed the holy link of matrimony. The son also shall be free for his hands are clean. Cerbio will be given the Kingdom and by his wise rule his father's guilt shall be atoned."

Nabor whose head had been bowed even deeper during the pronouncement of the verdict, was seized by great emotion upon hearing the acquittal of his friend. With the vision of Cerbio walking off into self-imposed exile before his mind's eye, he now wondered how one might hold him back: indeed, Nabor feared Cerbio might go against Huatami's decision and follow his father rather than ascend to the throne and so, notwithstanding the strictness of the ritual—he exclaimed, "Cerbio, together with his mother Hethara, want to share Kaana's lot!"

Surprised the Loki turned around. "Where did you see Cerbio?"

Nabor bowed his head and placed his hand across his heart. "I saw him, clad in rough clothing, with his parents outside the city gates of Bayagard, and, O Enlightened One, I also saw him at nightfall by the bridge leading to the Temple-Fortress."

Huatami clapped his hands and a subordinate priest appeared.

"Bring me Cerbio and Hethara!" the Loki commanded him. Silence returned to the Hall of Kings but this time the kings' faces were cheerful and it was as if a sigh of relief was passing through their ranks. Soon the priest returned announcing, "Those you wish to see, Sire, are in the inner court."

"Then open the curtain!"

Now the tall figure of the Priest-King became visible to all those crowding in the inner court. Huatami recognized Cerbio who was giving support to his mother.

"Come closer, Cerbio!" the Loki ordered him.

With some hesitation, the son let go of his mother and entered the circle of kings.

"In accordance to *Elohim*'s desire, I herewith appoint you Lucoman of Waya! Fulfill your duty—by which Kaana's guilt will be atoned!"

This statement was greeted by the Lucoman with a single, loud outcry of joy but Cerbio had turned as pale as death. Evidently, there was a struggle waging within him. As much as his father's crime was abhorrent to him, the son's young heart was still attached to him. The Priest-King was clearly aware of Cerbio's wavering, reflected in those young and open features. Huatami placed his hand on Cerbio's shoulder. "Yield to *Elohim*'s will! Think of Hethara! Why should she perish, too?" he said.

This decided the matter for Cerbio. He bowed deeply and Huatami blessed him, before putting his arms around the young prince and leading him up to the column of Waya. Cerbio's eyes were searching for his mother. Hethara was still standing in the crowd; a quiet glow shone in her eyes. Seeing her son, her cherished child, reestablished in his rightful position, she began murmuring prayers of gratitude. She knew now that all would be well again.

The news of these events spread like wildfire, breaking the evil spell the bloody deed had cast over the minds of the people. Passed along by word of mouth, the good tidings caused great joy everywhere. All were agreed that the Priest-King had passed a just judgment.

The midday sun lay heavily on Mayagard. Only a light breeze moved the fan-like branches of the palm-trees; it played with the flowers and leaves and swelled the curtains on the windows of the Palace. In her apartment Maya reclined on her couch, abandoned to her thoughts. At her feet a young cheetah playfully if a little clumsily—tried to tear off one of the tassels of her footrest. For a while the Lucoman delighted in observing the animal's attempts but then she drove it from the room somewhat roughly. Her thoughts turned back to her husband. She missed him. She missed his warmth, a warmth that used to envelop her with its gentle tenderness. He had never interfered with her wishes, had always been of an even friendliness—not only toward her but toward all people. She knew the people revered him. He had always been acclaimed jubilantly when he made a public appearance or participated in one of the races in the Arena. He loved singing and dancing. During public banquets in the Great Hall he often rose to his feet and danced to the sounds of the accompanying harps and flutes. Totally at ease at such occasions, his body would swing to the rhythm of the music. The smoothness and natural grace of his movements as well as the ecstatic joy on his young face captured everybody's attention and the applause he was given was not just a polite tribute. Maya had always been happy about this—and yet! At times, when Nabor had been floating through the large hall with astonishing grace, ease and abandonment, she had experienced a certain irritation at the realization that even the spectators were surprised; obviously for them it did not seem the most natural thing in the world that their ruler should engage in dancing with such passion.

"He has the strength of a bull, the suppleness of a cheetah and the grace of a woman"—these words by Mamya did not have a nice ring to her ears and whenever she remembered them she felt a sting. On the other hand, she was reconciled every time she saw Nabor driving his team-of-four at high speed through the Arena, his tall, slender figure looking the very image of manly strength, with his long shiny hair flowing in the wind. She lay there visualizing his profile cutting through the air like a finely sculptured eagle's head, his lips shut firmly, those shining eyes. It was this aspect of him that corresponded most to Maya's idea of a ruler and a man.

Suddenly her attention was caught by the sound of excited voices in the great yard of the Palace; soon her door was pushed open violently and Eseko, the old attendant, burst into the room sputtering forth, "There are a large number of ships approaching our coast, Milady!"

Maya sat up. "Ships?" She rose to her feet and left the room hastily. Eseko followed her up to the battlements and, indeed, there in the far distance on the blue, scintillating surface of the sea she saw tiny dots growing ever larger. When her eyes had become accustomed to looking into the distance, she was able to make out these dots as sailing ships. For a long time she stood there staring into the distance. When the ships had come close enough to shore, the Mayas could see many men upon the decks clad in animal skins and carrying long spears with pointed, glittering tips. The vessels were carried along swiftly by large powerful wind-swelled sails. Protected by round shields on their sides, a crew of oarsmen was squatted along the sides of the ships. When the largest of the galleys had come close enough one could make out a small tent-like structure on its deck under which a young man wearing gleaming bracelets on his arms was resting upon a fur-covered bed-like platform. Around him stood a few men, all dressed in deer-skins like himself, who—with their heads bowed and in an overall attitude of submission—appeared to listen to something he was telling them. Maya watched the scene with interest.

She directed most of her attention to that large ship, as she guessed the man on the fur-covered bed to be the chief of the armada. At one point she heard loud shouting and howling coming from the ships. She could see the men brandishing their spears and getting into a dance of joy reminiscent of the clumsy movements of the bears of the North. She smiled at the drollness of it all. Meanwhile the aliens had obviously discovered the entrance to the canal, as the largest of the vessels was definitely setting sail for it. All the ships that had so far sailed ahead of the chief's vessel stopped and moved to the rear of the convoy to follow the general movement.

"They're coming into the canal, Milady, what are we to do?" the official beside her asked. Maya turned her head. After some reflection she issued a short order: "Have the gates of the canal closed!"

Eseko left quickly, while Maya went to the side of the battlements that opened out on the canal. She saw the large boat glide closer. The man on the fur-covered bed had risen to his feet and moved to the rail. He was tall and muscular and dressed in a short doublet-like garment leaving his legs and arm bare; his raven-black hair, which had probably been oiled, was shining in the sunlight. He wore it pulled back and tied up in what appeared to be a knot. From the belt around his waist hung some glittering object on one side and, on the other, a small horn. His feet were wrapped in furs fastened to his lower calves by crossing straps. When Maya was able to make out the stranger's face, she noticed that he was quite young, clean-shaven and that his bushy eye-brows shaded eyes as dark as the night. Below his strong, prominent nose she noticed his defiant, energetic mouth, his full lips. His face, his overall attitude and his outlandish get-up gave the man an appearance somewhat reminiscent of a wild and reckless animal.

"A black panther," shot through her mind.

She heard steps approaching behind her. Eseko had come back.

"Milady," he said, "the foreigners are landing inside the canal and have begun to climb up the embankments."

The Lucoman turned pale: she knew those were wild people from the dark side of the Earth. According to the historical myths, those people had already once before brought great distress to Eya-Eya.

"Go to meet them and offer them my respects!" she ordered Eseko.

The old man was stunned; he hesitated. Then Maya had an idea. She signaled him to come closer and pointed at the man in the big boat.

"That man over there is the chief of the horde. Speak to him and bring him here!"

Eseko withdrew slowly, as if unsure. Maya continued observing the foreigner for a little longer then she, too, left the roof. Back in her apartments she ordered to her maids, "Adorn me!"

They put a large golden ruby-encrusted diadem on top of her hair like a crown. In her auburn curls the rubies glittered like drops of blood. She also wore rubies on her dress, her arms and her fingertips. The Lucoman stood tall and straight but her heart did not beat with ease. A sensation of danger had crept over her, nothing however in her facial expression betrayed her anxiety. The royal coat was put around her shoulders by officious hands. She stepped out into the throne hall and sat on the high throne around which the highest officials, stewards and chamberlains of the Kingdom were gathering.

An expectant tension hummed throughout the room. In her heart, Maya implored *Elohim* to let Nabor return to her soon. Then, suddenly, the confused noise of foreign voices was heard—

and almost immediately Eseko returned gesturing invitingly to someone behind him: the chief of the aliens entered the Hall. It was indeed the dark-haired young man from the big ship. He was followed by a group of bearded men whose heavy metal ornaments designated their high rank. The young chief moved with great self-assurance and ease but as soon as he saw Maya he stopped short in surprise. Her beauty and royal jewels had thrown him off his balance. Maya smiled softly—a smile which was followed by similar smiles on the faces of the courtiers.

The foreigner bent his knee before the surprised Lucoman who had never before been paid such homage. She rose and nodded her beautiful head as a gesture of salutation.

"Who are you, stranger?" she asked and the clear sound of her voice filled the Hall. The man looked confused: he had not understood her language. Maya looked across to Eseko for support and the old man began gesturing vividly to make the foreign chief grasp the meaning of her words. But the latter remained silent and only shook his head. Eseko tried again and again by pointing first to the visitor, then to Maya's courtiers and, finally to the sea. At last the man's tawny face lit up in comprehension and pointing to himself he said in a strange guttural tone: "Wea"—and again "Wea." Then he gestured toward his bearded companions saying, "Tursian."

"I see," Eseko said tentatively, "you are the king of the Tursians."

But the man only shrugged his shoulders. Then he turned toward his men and commanded them in a low voice to throw themselves down, touching the ground with their foreheads. The proud Wea looked back at Maya who answered him with another nod.

"My mistress, the Lucoman of the Mayan Kingdom, welcomes you as her guest," Eseko tried once more.

"Maya" the young king of the Tursians repeated. And again: "Maya."

He waved at one of his men who left the room hurriedly and soon returned with several other Tursians carrying bales of animal furs which they put down at Wea's feet. They opened the bales to display bracelets and rings made of some yellowish metal, belts embossed with metal, shiny short swords and various horns of all sizes. By a gesture with his hand Wea indicated that he wished to offer these objects to Maya. A nod of her regal head, which made the rubies glitter in her hair, showed him that she accepted his gifts with thanks.

While this silent ceremony of mutual paying of respect was running its course within the Palace, dramatic scenes were taking place in the streets of Mayagard: The Tursians, who had reached the town, were busy catching any and all the animals they could get hold of and were celebrating with a great slaughter orgy, in the course of which clashes with the owners of the animals had flared up. The foreigners were using their weapons and a number of the citizens of Mayagard had been injured. One of them, an elderly man who was bleeding from a gash on his head, came tumbling into the royal hall. With blood streaming down his face and dress he cried out, "Milady, these foreigners are striking our sons!"

Maya jumped to her feet, her eyes flashing in sudden anger.

"Your men are breaking the holy laws of hospitality!" she reprimanded Wea.

The latter stood in silence, disconcerted. Soon more wounded Mayans came in. An icy expression on her face, Maya pointed to these people and then to Wea's companions. At last he understood. His face became distorted with violent anger and with a harsh shout of command to his men he ran out of the room. Maya followed him with dreadful misgivings; she found him standing on the porch outside, the horn at his mouth emitting a dull, drawn-out sound that echoed off into the distance. At once Tursians came running from all sides. They looked up at their master and, seeing his wrath, they were filled with fear. Wea pointed wildly at the injured Mayans and his mighty voice rang out across the square, "You dogs! How dare you soil my honor?"

The men stood there, their heads drooped in shame.

"Who did this?" Wea shouted, but nobody stirred. The young chief was beside himself and just about to throw himself on those nearest to him when he became aware of Maya's presence.

He controlled himself and turned his attention to the wounded Mayas. They came up to him and, with the appropriate gestures, he demanded that they point out the culprits. Some complied with his demand and began walking up and down the rows of Tursians, pointing out the offenders.

Wea motioned to those who had been identified to come closer. They obeyed and—trembling with fear—threw themselves to the ground. Their chief looked down on them in his fury—and commanded to his officers, "Kill them!"

The culprits broke into shrill wailing as the officers drew swords from their leather sheaths in order to carry out the sentence. But when the first one lifted his arm to strike, a woman's voice cried out: it was Maya. Wea swirled round and all his men stared at the Lucoman.

"Stop, Wea! For holy is a man's life to the Atlanteans," she exclaimed, waving her arm in an attempt to stop the executioners.

Taken a-back, Wea looked up at her. At this moment, in her magnificent beauty she seemed to him like a supernatural being. He nodded silently; he had understood. One short signal with his hand and his officers put their swords back into their sheaths. The Lucoman turned around and returned to her Palace. Eseko came up to Wea and led him to a large complex of buildings in which he and his men were given accommodations.

Meanwhile, Bayagard was filled with unbridled euphoria as the Night of Light led from one feast to another. Herio, the Lucoman of Baya, used all means at his disposal to sweeten the days for his guests and organized all manner of games, dances, cruises on the canals and along the sea-shore. All these events culminated in a great chariot race which was won by Cerbio. Cheered on by many thousands of people and adorned with garlands of flowers, he returned to his Palace at the head of a procession of Lucoman.

There was the tradition in Atlantis that the Lucoman would gather in working committees to discuss questions of legislation, voting all suggested amendments by simple majority. In the case of a split vote, the Priest-King was called upon to break the tie. It was in the light of this tradition that the Lucoman had come together again in the Hall of Kings of the Temple. The Loki had taken the floor and was addressing the kings on the principles of high idealism and only briefly touched upon problems relating to external affairs. The general substance of his speech was the moral attitude of the Atlanteans. He proclaimed,

"You will be responsible to *Elohim* for the well-being of your people. If you live in purity, your subjects also will live in purity. If you stand up for justice, injustice will not have an opportunity. If your words are true and correspond to your actions, you will be a true model to those governed by you. You must keep this in mind always! We, the elite, must remember this just as much as our subjects. You are called upon—indeed, you have been elected—to walk ahead of the people as bearers of Light."

After these words Huatami blessed each one of them and when he left the Hall all the Lucoman paid him his due respect.

Carriages with teams-of-four brought the rulers back to the Palace where a banquet awaited them. Soon they were lying on couches and chatting with one another. Servants offered fruits and sparkling jeweled cups filled with delicious wine. Harps were playing, songs rang out, flutes tweeted enticing melodies answered by oboes and cymbals. Dancers appeared in costumes of heavy silk, richly embroidered with precious stones. Moving with solemn steps and keeping their faces as rigid as masks in which their eyes shone with ecstatic fire, they personified the Sons of Light. Then dancing girls in airy frocks scurried into the scene. They began whirling around the solemn Sons of Light, enticing them by billowing this way and that. The Sons of Light resisted them for some time but then, gradually captured by the enrapturing movements of the maidens, gave in to their rhythm one after the other. Eventually the harps and flutes stopped; only the oboes and cymbals continued to sustain the delirious whirl in which all the dancers had finally been caught. But then, suddenly, the full sound of a gong was heard: once..., twice..., thrice and—as if charmed by a spell—the dancers froze in statuesque poses. At that moment a small figure, dressed in garments seemingly made of light, came hovering into the room and the music came to an abrupt halt—and all the dancing girls humbly withdrew from the scene.

Again the flutes began, again harps were heard, again festive songs rang out as the Being of Light guided home the Sons of Light, its companions.

During all this Nabor had been sitting on the lower end of his father's couch. He had been completely transfixed by the dancing and the music. Himself a passionate dancer, he had savored the performance with all the elements of his sensuous mind. His nerves were tingling: how much he would have loved to be one of the dancers himself, but....

Ebor, his father, was surreptitiously observing his son. How different he was from his oldest one! How much he resembled his mother in his physical beauty! The perfect proportions of his body went hand in hand with his charming movements. How willing he always was to serve others, to comply with their wishes. But was he the man to rule a great kingdom—would he be a match to the task? Nabor loved beauty and harmony; he would rather avoid all hardship. He had received the same education as his older brother, drove a coach of four, was able to handle horses well, swam and rowed just as well as his brother, but it was obvious that he did all those things without any real mettle. There was no ambition in him that might have driven him to truly brilliant achievements. If he was leading in a sporting event, he always tended to hold back just before reaching the goal and to let others win in his stead.

Ebor was so deeply immersed in his thoughts that the Chamberlain standing behind him had to clear his throat several times to get his attention,

"What is it?" Ebor finally said.

"Nabor and Cerbio are to come to the Temple in the early morning. This is a message the Loki is sending you," was the answer.

Just then the dance came to an end and the applause was swelling up as Nabor—his face aglow with enthusiasm—turned to his father. The latter looked at him sternly and said,

"The Priest-King orders you and Cerbio in the Temple."

"What could he want?" Nabor asked in surprise.

"It is about the initiation, my son. You know, only Lucoman and priests may receive it. Mysteries which grant you power over others will be revealed to you but beware of misusing your power. Unspeakable misery will come over those *Elohim*, in his Mercy, has chosen from among his people but who prove an undeserving vessel of His will! Never forget this: power tastes sweeter than the sweetest fruit and is more intoxicating than the most delicious of wines!"

At dawn, just when the brilliant sun was rising out of the ocean, the two young princes arrived at the Temple's gates. A cool breeze was coming in from the sea as they pulled their royal cloaks in more tightly around their bodies. None of them spoke but their young hearts were beating anxiously.

At last the gold-plated gates opened and a group of priests stood there before them, amongst whom was Tenupo and who greeted them thus:

"Enter, your royal Highnesses, *Elohim*'s grace be with you!"

They crossed the fore-court and arrived at the Hall of Kings. Upon a sign from Tenupo, the curtain isolating the Holy chamber opened noiselessly and they saw the Loki standing in the far background. Both Lucoman greeted him, according to custom, with their hands opened outward and held up to their foreheads in such a fashion that their thumbs and forefingers formed a triangle.

"Welcome to *Elohim*'s Hall," he said in a voice so soft and kind that all their shyness vanished at once.

"You have been chosen to be leaders in Eya-Eya's blessed lands. However, in order to preserve this great blessing, you must become ego-less. The higher a human being, the greater the burden he is given to carry upon his shoulders, the more important the responsibilities before his god and his people. He who wants to rule others must first learn to rule himself. You must forsake your "I" and dissolve into the "Thou." The Path that leads to the Light is hard and steep. You will be shown the way in three times seven days; during this time you will—after having undergone a spiritual transformation—be connected to the Ring of Light. Are you ready to walk the difficult road of the initiation?"

The two princes bent their heads in silence.

"Then open your hearts so that they may be filled with the Great Spirit's grace enabling them to give up their self-existence by becoming vessels of Light!"

Huatami closed his eyes and a softly glowing golden light could be seen shining around him.

Tenupo accompanied the Lucoman out of the room. They were not permitted to remain together; each of them was given a separate narrow and barren cell as a dwelling place. Tenupo instructed them in how to control their breath and how to silence the inner mental chatter. Their daily food consisted only of some fruit and water—but even these frugal meals were gradually reduced to a simple pitcher of water. It was less difficult for Cerbio to fast than for Nabor, who was tortured by the desire for the pleasures of the palate he had been used to in the past. It took all his willpower to calm down his rebellious stomach and it took three entire days before the will of his body was broken at last. He followed his breathing exercises and mind-silencing practices in obedience. Tenupo came to see his disciples several times a day. He anointed them and laid his hand on their foreheads to fortify them. After the first seven days the two young men were free from all desire; pale and emaciated, they reclined on their wooden beds.

At this point the rhythmical breathing exercises were intensified in the supervising presence of the High Priest. Slowly the loosening of the connection with the body began. By the second day, Nabor became aware of a dull pressure in the area of his navel—after which there was something like a gentle pull and, simultaneously, a strangling sensation—and then—he was out of his body. A dim light seemed to surround him and he saw himself lying on his plank bed. Nearby he saw Tenupo surrounded by a light brighter than his. Around them a great darkness prevailed—and, just as he began to experience fear, Tenupo's light enveloped him and he felt wonderfully united with him, practically drowning in the luminous radiation emitted by the teacher. Then Tenupo withdrew—and, once again, Nabor perceived a sensation of fear. At that moment a thought entered his mind: *Elohim*—and the following instant he found himself back in his body. A soft groan escaped his lips and as he sat up he saw Tenupo's kind face smiling at him.

"You have passed the first test, Nabor! Now you know that your body is only one of the physical sheaths that you can use or leave at your own discretion."

Nabor managed a tired nod; he was shaken to his very core. Tenupo blessed his student and withdrew.

Cerbio, on the other hand, kept struggling in vain. Again and again he exerted himself to keep his breath in the necessary three-phased harmony but nightmares assailed him each time and he lost his grasp on the exercise. Pictures and events of his young life kept surging up, beings that seemed to have arisen out of dim dreams kept him fettered; he was not once able to reach the stillness of the holy ones.

Tenupo attempted to assist him: "Your soul is filled with the swelling glow of your young existence! Don't torture yourself, my son, if you can't reach the gate to the vast expanses of the light-filled realms, be content to remain with the knowledge you have so far received—until, one day, the shackles binding you to this world will at last be loosened."

"But—Nabor? Did he find the Path?" Cerbio inquired shyly.

"He found it after much effort," the priest replied. "But he had already been equipped previously with the capacity to reach the highest point of ecstasy. That is why, this time, he was able to leave his body's narrow sheath. His faith is strong and his heart is soft. If he reaches the end of the Path he will be a guiding light for all the sons of Eya-Eya."

The High Priest had come once again to see Nabor in his cell. The presence of the teacher made the pupil forget all the hardships of the inner struggle. Tenupo sat down beside him and wisdom began to flow from his lips—a wisdom, the young adept took in hungrily.

Tenupo said, "He who walks the right path, my friend, will be taken by the hand and led forward. But what is the right path and who are those upon it? In your innermost core there is a voice which tells you, without failure, whether you are on the right path or not! To be able to hear that softly ringing, bell-like voice is the condition for finding the right path. When you are in doubt, just listen within! As long as you let yourself be carried ahead by peace and inner equilibrium, if harmony fills you and you feel the certainty that nothing can harm you, you are on the right path. But if you have gone astray, there is restlessness inside you and anguish fills your heart. Then you see clouds everywhere, you see disaster everywhere. In such moments you must know that you have made a mistake somewhere and you should repent. In other words, if you have done something wrong, recognize it as such and change your ways even if that should mean going against your pride, humbling yourself.

Silence is necessary for he who immerses himself into himself in order to discover his pristine forces. Silence will snatch us out of the bustle of the world, it will envelop us, isolate us from others and enable us to listen within. Hence, train yourself to be silent! But you must be careful not to ponder over your own mind in a complacent sort of way, Nabor! Listen to your inner voice in all humility, asking it to guide you. Speak to it and say, "Guide me out of the narrowness, out of this darkness and make me recognize those who, like brothers, are on the same road as I. Make a bell resound inside me, a bell admonishing me every time I lose my way. Don't remain silent, O you my Inner Voice, for my ear wants to hear you and my feet want to follow you. Guide me to the Light!"

These lofty thoughts were hovering in the room and replenishing Nabor's soul but Tenupo continued, "Look here, Nabor! We all have to struggle—day after day. Your struggle will not be over after this short period of initiation. Even a man who has attained wisdom still feels the thirst for existence inside him. I am telling you this so you will continue to exert yourself and not commit an error so common in this world and think that you won't be able to do this or that because you are fettered by old habits. I tell you: try and try again! Don't consider your "*I*," consider the "*thou*." "*Thou*"—that is everybody who crosses your path. Be truthful and unselfish, for all selfishness must be paid for! Be just—not only toward yourself but toward all those who are on the road of this life with you—those, I mean, you have the obligation to include into your life and have no right to exclude! Sometimes this is a difficult test for us, I know, but there is no way leading upward that could be trodden without a struggle and each gate that opens up before us must be conquered by means of a sacrifice—and there are many gates as yet blocking our road. Don't forget that! Be sure to pledge all your love to *Elohim* and promise Him that you will never leave the Path leading up to Him, and may this love take you to His heart so that He will let you enter His Kingdom of Light when the moment has arrived."

Nabor felt the old priest's hand pressing his softly—then withdrawing from the clasp. He heard light steps, the subdued noise of the curtain closing—and silence enveloped him again. It was a solemn silence and all he had just been told was throbbing, as if alive, in his innermost being, moving his heart.

It was night. Nabor was lying on his hard bed as rigidly as a corpse. Pale moonlight shone into his narrow abode and a distant smile lingered upon his lean face: he had withdrawn within. His breathing was barely perceptible, all his senses were directed inward. He was filled with a deep and nostalgic yearning. Would the dark veil tear asunder? Suddenly—somewhere in the very far distance—a point of light could be seen on the horizon…but almost at once it disappeared again. Then it was there anew—only closer and stronger now—and, finally, shone forth from all sides. There was light all around him like some incandescent fire—in fact, it was all coming from *within* him. He felt himself floating in an ocean of light—an ocean of light with a central point toward which he was headed and with which, at last, he became one.

He was looking into some limitless distance, into a space filled with blazing light in which countless beings of rare beauty and with wonderful faces kept moving hither and thither. Those closest to him were looking at him and approached closer still. They gazed at him with their big eyes shining with kindness. Suddenly, at a great distance in this light-filled space, a golden ray flashed forth and passed through him like a bolt. There was just enough time for him to see these myriad beings turning back toward that light before he came out of his absorption abruptly. He opened his eyes and while he was still under the impact of what he had just experienced, the curtain moved and Tenupo entered the room.

"I beheld a wonderful world full of wonderful beings as numberless as the sand on the shore of the sea," Nabor stammered, as happy as a child.

"I know you did," the priest replied to Nabor's surprise; Tenupo even made a comment: "Whenever I connect with your consciousness I can experience your experiences."

"Where is that magnificent kingdom?" Nabor wanted to know.

"It's the Realm of Light enveloping the Earth. Our planet is embedded in that Realm like a kernel in a fruit. You had penetrated the consciousness of your mind, whose light was thus able to surge forth and break through the darkness, to carry you up. In this way you were granted a view of your light-filled homeland where you will return after the duties of this earthly existence have been fulfilled."

"I saw a light shining more golden than the sun and stronger than lightning. There were beings who turned toward me. It was too much for me. I am shaken to the core!"

Tenupo's face showed respectful surprise. He bowed to Nabor, still lying on his bed, and whispered into his ear very softly,

"The highest mystery has been revealed to you, you blessed youth! What you saw was the Golden Light of the Logos' world."

"The Logos' world? Who is the Logos?" Nabor asked shyly.

"*Elohim*, the Highest One, is omnipresent. It is not possible for our minds to understand or to realize His greatness even in the minutest degree. The Logos is the only son of the Father-of-All. He is the Highest after Him. He is the ruler over innumerable realms; the planet Earth is also under his government." The priest continued, "May your mouth remain silent! Don't ever mention what you have seen. The time to reveal the Logos' might has not yet come. But you were chosen to protect the Empire our forefathers created. At present, the Dark Ones are gathering in the East, they have no knowledge of the Light's wonderful power and of *Elohim*'s holy laws."

It seemed to Nabor that something like the icy wind which precedes impending danger had passed across his soul. And, indeed, Tenupo added,

"Once before, we suffered unspeakable misery through the Dark Ones' low being. You must know, son of Ebor, that in the same way the mosaic-colored headband encircles a Lucoman's head, the globe of the Earth used to be encircled by the unimaginable beauty of the Kingdom of *Elohim*'s Sons. Our forebears' days were filled with *Elohim*'s splendor because they were connected to the Empire of Light that our inner senses are given to perceive. Those forefathers of ours had bodies shining with light-filled beauty—bodies they left and assumed again at their own discretion. Beings of Light came to them and they were able to visit the Beings of Light. Heaven and Earth were one. Our forefathers would not walk upon, but hover above, the Earth, they had not yet acquired any mass. They worshipped *Elohim* in holy groves. The twelve holy couples whose statues you can see standing in front of our temples were the ancestors of our twelve peoples. Those royal couples must have lived for about a thousand years in Asgard, their fortress, which reached up to the very sky. The twelve individual empires as we know them today were founded much later—each with its own Palace-Fortress named after their respective countries. In those days the stars could not be seen in the blazing light streaming forth uninterruptedly from the Empire of Light and flooding the Atlantean Ring. The spiritual guide for that entire world was the Logos—a world condition which lasted until the day three beings of great beauty—descendants of the Dark Ones abiding outside the Atlantean Ring—entered that Ring. Their hair was as black as night, they wore garments made of rough cloth and they knew nothing of the existence of gold and splendor. What they were knowledgeable about, however, was the art of brewing fermented drinks. They knew about trees, the fruits of which they used for making their intoxicating beverages. Our forefathers quickly learned this art from them and began to drink that brew to the point of inebriety so that those whose minds had been so clear before now became befuddled. The Law which had been engraved into their hearts was clogged up and buried. They lost the gift of vision and inner audition and became like those alien beings.

At the same time—a time at which three thousand generations were incarnated simultaneously—the first Loki was appointed. From that moment forth, he alone received the Laws which had so far been a part of everybody's natural consciousness. That first Loki lay face-down for three days because he could not bear *Elohim*'s brilliant Light. On the spot where he had lain he erected the Temple-Fortress you can still see today.

But then another catastrophe occurred: The Earth passed through the tail of the comet Cronos which was traveling through our solar system. Blazing fires and masses of scalding water transfigured the face of the Earth. The great Empire of our forefathers was destroyed. Only Eya-Eya remained as it is today, surrounded by warm oceanic streams. It was here that those who were considered pure established our new homeland. The cataclysm had torn asunder the cloud cover which had previously enveloped and protected the Atlantean kingdoms. The sun and the moon became visible but the Light from *Elohim*'s Empire ceased to shine. For the first time one could see a rainbow. Lot, the first Loki, who had—together with those who had kept their faith in *Elohim*—survived the cataclysm, saw this new phenomenon and knelt down before it. He gave thanks for his rescue and took the rainbow as a symbol which—shaped like a bridge as it were and reaching beyond the atmosphere of the Earth—stood for a new alliance. Since that time, the Loki alone has been the keeper of the connection with the Empire of Light. He is *Elohim*'s vessel, he receives the divine commandments and passes them along for the benefit of all Atlanteans."

Tenupo stopped speaking. Silence reigned in the narrow dwelling. Nabor's entire being was in turmoil. The thought of the fate of his forebears fell across his soul like an oppressive shadow.

"Will I be strong enough to understand the Dark One?" he asked in anguish.

"You must train yourself to act as *Elohim*'s deserving tool. If you continue on this path you will become aware of the great strength within you and in hours of danger great power will be yours." Tenupo's eyes locked with his. Nabor's heart was beating nervously, contradictory emotions were struggling within his chest. How beautiful life had been so far but now, all of a sudden, inscrutable shadows were threatening to plunge it into darkness and—as he now knew—it was his task to repel these dangers!

For a long time he lay on his bed, churning these thoughts over and over again in his mind. Then, in the silence of the night, he heard his own voice say, "As it seems to be *Elohim*'s will, so be it!"

"Indeed, it is His will," Tenupo solemnly declared. "The hour of your trial of strength is near!"—and having blessed Nabor, he left.

The period of the initiation was drawing to a close and priests brought back Nabor's royal apparel before leading him back to the Hall of Kings. Soon Cerbio arrived and he thrust his arms around Nabor with a cry of joy, but then he looked at him with searching eyes. What he saw was a pale and emaciated face, with eyes set deep in their sockets but illuminated by an hitherto unknown light. Cerbio, too, looked worn but he was glad that the days of the initiation were over. His questions gushed forth, however. Nabor said nothing at first. Only when Cerbio insisted he calmly replied, "You know all about it—so why do you ask me?"

Puzzled, Cerbio stepped back. How changed Nabor was! So serious and quiet, he hardly recognized his formerly cheerful companion. The two friends were given a solemn and ceremonious farewell: the Loki blessed them and addressed them like a kind father. He pulled Nabor closer to him and whispered in his ear, "Your path will be difficult! Treasure *Elohim*'s memory and be mindful of the strength that became alive within you!"

Meanwhile, the alien guests kept the citizens of Mayagard in a constant state of agitation. Day after day they gathered in small groups and went into the forests and groves to hunt and kill animals which, until now, had been living and grazing there in peace. They barbecued the killed deer over an open fire on one of their spears. Again and again they filled their drinking horns. Singing was heard—a singing in harsh tones, provocative in both tune and rhythm. Their dances were just a wild leaping around an open fire.

Apart from a small number of servants who struck up friendships with the Tursians, all the noble Mayas kept their distance. The old Eseko, however, endeavored to teach Wea the Atlantean language. The Tursian proved a zealous pupil but his tongue—used to guttural sounds—managed to reproduce only a distorted version of the Atlantean words. At the same time, the old steward introduced him to the way-of-life of the Mayan social elite.

By now, Wea was in the habit of dressing in precious silk robes sent to him by Maya. He wore his hair Atlantean style, parted in the middle with curls all around his head. His golden headband, his robe and his hands were adorned with precious jewelry. When he appeared before Maya so attired for the first time, she was stunned by his exotic beauty. She listened with amusement to the short speech he gave her in her own language, although it rolled off his tongue only in broken and heavy sounds. Her reply was friendly,

"The happiness of my guests is also my happiness."

Then she showed him around the palace. The Tursian expressed his admiration as exuberantly as a young child. Looking at precious cups and dishes, touching magnificent, multicolored silk cushions, he ran this way and that. Although he was interested in everything, he was particularly taken by the artfully cut wooden chests and coffers. His enthusiastic cries were filled with questions that Maya did her best to answer. Eventually, a meal consisting of delicious pastry, many different fruits and well laced with wine concluded the visit—which was to be followed by many more.

The Lucoman was nervously walking the floor of her chamber. She had been waiting for her husband for weeks. A few days previously she had sent a messenger on horseback to Bayagard, demanding Nabor's return. She was wondering what might have happened in Bayagard; after all, the Festival of Light was long over.

Just then the curtain was pulled aside, a servant in dusty clothes entered and said, bowing deeply, "Milady, the Lucoman is staying at the Loki's Temple-Fortress together with Cerbio, Kaana's son. Nobody is allowed to see them."

So that was it! Nabor and Cerbio were the Loki's guests! But what did it all mean? Maya turned these thoughts over and over in her mind—then she addressed the patient messenger,

"Fetch Amatur, the priest!"

The man left and she walked over to one of the windows and stared out into the distance with unseeing eyes. The priests were probably trying to get him, the devout man, totally under their influence with the intention of ruling the Mayan Kingdom through him—against her will, of course! She bit her lower lip hard. The memory of Huatami, humbling her pride and breaking her will, had returned. A contemptuous twitch flicked across her mouth as her thoughts returned to her husband. Maya saw Nabor as a dreamer, as someone like wax in the priests' elegant hands. She had become afraid of Nabor's faith; she knew that in Nabor's eyes the Loki was truly *Elohim*'s go-between and everyone had to submit to him. She recalled Nabor's uncomprehending look when she had tried to shake him out of his conviction. Suddenly her brooding was interrupted by a rustling movement behind her.

"You called me, Milady?" Amatur, a beardless young man, greeted her. He looked at her expectantly. Pointing to an armchair, the Lucoman bid him to take a seat. Then, as she herself stretched out on her couch, she said slowly,

"My husband has not returned." She looked at the priest from under half-closed eyelids, "The Loki is keeping him as a guest in the Temple-Fortress."

"That is a great honor for his Majesty, the Lucoman," Amatur replied. His face remained inscrutable, however, and Maya tried in vain to read in his perfectly controlled features.

Then she said with a smile, "An honor—yes. But why is this honor granted only to Nabor and Cerbio, the two youngest of the Lucoman?"

"Cerbio, the son of Kaana, a Lucoman?" Amatur asked, avoiding a straight answer.

"That is what my messenger said," Maya replied curtly.

"Then," Amatur guessed, "he must have been elevated by the grace of Huatami!"

"The grace of Huatami!" Maya's forehead twisted into a deep frown but then she added, "Of course it is right not to make the son pay for the father's sins, but why is Huatami keeping my husband?"

Her tone of voice had become hostile. A chilly glint flashed up in the priest's eyes when he said, "It is not for me to judge Huatami's actions. You must ask Nabor, Milady, when he returns."

Maya rose to her feet slowly. Proudly she said, "Your council, priest, does nothing to soothe the worries of my heart. I have called you in vain."

"You are worrying for no reason, Milady. Nabor is safe in the Enlightened One's Fortress where he is waited upon by *Elohim*'s servants." Amatur bowed to her and withdrew.

"*Elohim*'s servants are waiting upon him!" Maya repeated to herself. "They who rule through serving and who turn rulers into their servants," she thought rebelliously.

Suddenly trumpets were sounding in the distance. The sound came closer and grew louder. The Lucoman heard it with surprise. Her astonishment grew when all the other towers' trumpets gave their drawn-out answer. A chamberlain entered announcing, "The train of the Lucoman is nearing the city!"

A joyful pang went through Maya: Nabor was coming back; all was well now! She picked up a rod and struck a metal basin hanging from the ceiling. The sound could be heard in the entire Palace. Chambermaids came running, palace attendants followed suit.

"Let us give a fitting welcome to our lord!" Maya ordered them.

They all hurried away again, only a few chambermaids remaining with the Queen. Maya abandoned herself to their experienced hands, spurring them on with encouragement as they adored her.

Crowds began thronging in the streets. Everybody wanted to express their joy to Nabor at his return. To thank them he only smiled at them quietly. He was leading the horses himself; in the crowded roads his chariot advanced with difficulty. The train of royal carriages was now nearing the Temple. On the front steps stood Amatur and other priests to welcome their ruler. Nabor stopped the chariot and nodded to greet them. Amatur stepped forward from the group of priests and coming up to Nabor, he said: "*Elohim* bless your return home, your Majesty!" His voice was low and his gaze scrutinized Nabor's tall figure. The priest's interest was aroused: something in the Lucoman's eyes and bodily attitude struck him as different. He had seen that magical glow in other eyes before! In whose? Suddenly he remembered: Tenupo! The day the High Priest united Maya and the Lucoman in the holy bond of marriage he had had the same eyes. Amatur was aware of the meaning of this: "It is the glow of the Anointed Ones, of those initiated within. It is always by the light in the eyes one can recognize those who have become one with the light-filled realms of *Elohim*," his own teacher, an old priest, had once told him.

He looked again—more closely. "Yes, that's it!" he thought, and filled with awe he bowed his head deeply. Nabor was aware of the reason for this singular behavior with unaccustomed clarity. His gaze took hold of the priest like a light wave, enveloping and warming. Amatur for his part, was spellbound. His lips moved but no sound was to be heard. Eventually Nabor was able to make out the following words: "Thanks be to *Elohim* for granting me the grace to see the face of the Anointed One!"

Meanwhile the other carriages had also pulled up and all the courtiers became witnesses to this surprising scene. When Amatur spoke again, he said, "A sinister cloud has appeared, Sire! Dark-colored foreigners have come out of the sea like a swarm of fluttering bats and are pushing forth into our land."

A painful sting went through Nabor's heart: the dark danger had arrived already! Controlling his voice, he asked, "Where are those foreigners?"

"The Lucoman received them as her guests, Sire. They were given accommodation in the lodging houses of your palace attendants and servants."

Nabor's gaze went out into the distance. "The hour of your trial is near," he heard Tenupo's voice saying, and a determined expression appeared on his emaciated features. He thanked Amatur briefly and the chariots were set in motion again. Approaching the Palace, Nabor suddenly caught sight of some of the dark foreigners. Dressed either in a short outfit of rough material or in short-cut frocks of deer-skin, Wea's warriors hung around sitting or standing in small groups. A great number of dark eyes, filled with curiosity, turned their gaze toward the approaching carriages.

Nabor also saw the slightly bent figure of Eseko coming forward from the largest of the servants quarters and moving up to him swiftly. Executing a gesture of submission Eseko solemnly declared, "Seeing you, Sire, causes our hearts to rejoice."

"I understand that the sea has brought us uninvited guests."

"They are Tursians, Sire. They arrived here by boat from the East, the direction of the rising sun. Their king, by the name of Wea, is a guest of Milady's. She ordered us to treat him like an Eya-Eya Lucoman. Do you wish me to bring him before you?"

"When the sun sinks back into the ocean and *Elohim*'s Light fills the sky, I will call the foreigner to appear before me!"

Eseko stepped back and Nabor continued on his way.

A majestically adorned Maya stood on the uppermost step of the palace's front stairs and awaited her husband's return. Her heart was beating and her breath irregular: she was hardly able to control her nervousness. At last the procession of chariots appeared on the majestic palm-bordered boulevard which approached the palace from the other side of town. From her elevated position Maya was soon able to see Nabor—and a shock went through her: how pale he was! How serious his emaciated face! Only his eyes were shining with a peculiar brilliance.

He waved up at her, handed the reigns to his charioteer and stepped down from his carriage. Having hurried up the stairs, he gathered her in his arms. Instantly a great calmness enveloped her; cuddling up against him like a child, she enjoyed the gentle stroking of his tender hands.

"Maya," he said softly, and again, "Maya."

Coming from his lips, her name sounded like the theme of some mysterious hymn, some all-encompassing chant. Hand in hand they entered the palace. In the main hall, Maya put her hands on Nabor's shoulders and, looking at him directly she said deliberately, "Many days and nights have passed since you set out for the Lucoman Council's meeting…."

Nabor nodded, "The days in Bayagard flowed on like a beautiful dream and the nights were full of Light." Saying this, the brilliance of his eyes intensified and a blissful smile illuminated his features. Maya observed this transformation with astonishment; she began to realize that *something* had taken possession of Nabor's soul, something unknown to her, something she had no part of.

"Foreigners have come into the country," she said unhappily.

Nabor's glance came back to her and he said softly, "I know, Maya. I have already invited them to the palace for a festive dinner, tonight."

⁂

In the land of Eya-Eya hot springs spouted to the surface of the earth in many different places. The Atlanteans constructed their bath-houses around these geysers. The bath-houses themselves were large circular buildings made of marble with large apertures at all sides serving as windows and an open roof. Such facilities could be found scattered all over the flourishing countryside. Inside the bath-houses, around the hot spring proper, a large basin was usually installed into which the hot water from the spring, gushing forth in glittering cascades, was captured. The large hall housing the fountain was always filled with white steam; attendants and masseurs offered their services in the area around the basin, where couches were set up for the bathers to rest.

Having returned home, Nabor had gone to pay a visit to the bath-house connected to the Palace by a covered arcade. After some time Mamya had entered the steam-filled hall and begun pacing up and down, waiting for the Lucoman, when a servant approached him saying, "His Majesty is resting and has fallen asleep!" The Chamberlain nodded and went back to the Great Hall of the Palace where Premenio was directing the preparations for the festive banquet scheduled for that evening.

Servants were industriously spreading heavy purple carpets over the white marble floor. Along the walls, comfortable couches had been arranged. These sofas were covered with purple silk cushions, embellished with silver edges and tassels which underscored the dark shimmering hue of the pillows. At the upper end of each of these couches low, round marble tables had been placed, upon which stood small onyx dishes filled with fragrant flowers. The torches made of almond wood and drenched with olive oil were attached in large golden rings fixed high up on the walls and would spread a pleasant perfume as soon as they were lit. In flat dishes, supported by as many tripods, charcoal fires were already burning and in due time frankincense would be added to their glowing fire, thus making the air in the vast Hall redolent with balmy perfume.

When Premenio saw Mamya he exclaimed in a teasing tone of voice, "Where are you going, great master? Why so serious? Did your Sire disappear into the vapors of the bath-house?"

"When the Lucoman is taken into Lady Sleep's arms, he has no need of me, however loyally I might want to serve him!" Mamya replied with a smile.

"It seems to me" Premenio laughed, "that it would be the loyal servant's duty to watch over his ruler's sleep."

"Don't worry, our Lord is in good hands. Ekloh, the Rayanean attendant is a trusty guardian," Mamya answered, already on his way to her highness, the Lucoman.

He found her on the roof. Reclining on a couch under a canopy protecting her from the scorching sun, she lay daydreaming, gazing absentmindedly into the azure blue of the sky.

Mamya walked up to her softly. Maya turned her head. "Where is the Lucoman?" she asked.

"He fell asleep after his bath, Milady," Mamya said, smiling with devotion.

Maya propped her head up with her right hand. Her green shining eyes turned fully on the Chamberlain as she asked with emphasis, "What happened to Nabor? Don't you think, too, that he has changed?"

"Yes, the Lucoman has changed, as you say, Milady," Mamya admitted hesitatingly.

"Go on! I want to hear your opinion!" Maya ordered him.

"His Majesty has become so quiet…," Mamya broke off as if searching for the right words.

"And…?" Maya asked inquisitively.

"…and so aloof," Mamya concluded tentatively, adding after a moment's silence, "There is this special light in his eyes now." He stopped speaking but Maya gestured him to continue. He complied but gave his opinion very cautiously, "Something extraordinary must have happened for such a cheerful person as Nabor, who enjoyed life's pleasures so much, to turn into such a quiet man." Again he fell silent and looked at the Lucoman as if at a loss for words.

Maya bit her lower lip. "He is right," she thought, "a different Nabor has returned home—a grown-up man, somebody who underwent some deep transformation. When he left he was a youth but upon his return he has become a grave man."

"Whatever may have caused this?" the Lucoman wondered to herself.

Mamya shrugged his shoulders.

"Tell me what happened behind the walls of Bayagard!" Maya bid him and Mamya spoke to her of the celebrations and festivities and the Holy Night of Light. He told her about Cerbio's exculpation and elevation—but of course he knew nothing about the events which came to pass later, within the Temple's walls.

Maya listened sullenly; there was not the slightest ray of light in what he said that might help her to penetrate the darkness of the mystery that seemed to prevail here.

"Please go, Mamya!" she said tersely.

Mamya managed a forced smile and was already turning to leave when he stopped in his movement: a thought had struck him. He came closer once again. "The priests of Mayagard welcomed His Majesty on the stairs of the Temple," he said in a lively tone. Maya pricked up her ears—and finally sat up with keen interest when she learned of the meeting between Nabor and Amatur and she heard about Amatur's puzzling behavior.

"Amatur!" she said and—her shoulders dropping with discouragement—she added, "Amatur's made up his mind to tell me nothing." She signaled Mamya to take his leave.

"They stick together, those priests," she thought grimly, suddenly convinced that no one ever penetrated their secrets—and that even Nabor had been enslaved by them now. Huatami's power was definitely reaching right into her bedchamber and he proved strong enough to alienate from her what was dearest to her: her husband. Indeed, the Priest-King had prevailed over her twice: his verdict had taken her Kingdom away from her and his influence had deprived her of her husband who—until then—had been devoted to her so deeply and exclusively that she had hardly noticed the loss of political power caused by his ascension to the throne.

Reflecting on these facts, beautiful Maya lay on her couch tossing this way and that. Like a prisoner in a golden cage, the sides of which were closing in on her, suffocating her, Maya was nursing feelings of deep bitterness in her heart. It all felt like a nightmare. She needed a clear answer and decided to ask Nabor himself. But would he answer her questions, would he explain himself fully? Eventually she could not bear to lie there any longer. She rose with a jolt and quickly walked to the edge of the roof.

"How beautiful it is, this world! I want to be free. I want to wield power! I want to live in splendor!" She held her arms out as if to call the sun to her rescue. Slowly her inner tension relaxed. There!—hadn't she heard a noise? Frightened, she turned around...but nobody was there. She moved quickly to the steps leading into the interior of the Palace. She looked down—but saw nothing. Calm again, she returned to her couch and let herself sink into the pillows. She felt tender hands caressing her face; her sensuous lips whispered yearningly, "Nabor...."

The Great Hall of the Palace was bright with the light of many torches burning with a softly crackling sound. Their flickering glow was refracted by the marble walls and reflected back into the room, where the light rays touched the carpets, curtains and cushions, intensifying the dark purple color wherever they found it. The light scintillated off silver edges, fringes and tassels. Meanwhile, the open ceiling offered a magnificent view of the night sky, lit up by a myriad of dazzling stars.

The two throne-like seats for the royal couple stood upon a slightly elevated carpeted platform. One color—purple—dominated the large room, giving it a regal and resplendent atmosphere. In the adjacent rooms, separated from this Great Hall by curtains, musicians were tuning their instruments and both male and female dancers awaited the moment of their appearance on stage. Attendants were scurrying this way and that, carrying large platters of fruits—pineapple, oranges, grapes, bananas, dates, figs and nuts of various sizes. All shapes and manner of pastry made of rice flour were heaped on dishes, wine was ready to be served from golden pitchers.

At last the huge gong by the entrance issued its clamorous sound and the courtiers entered, attired in festive robes and followed by the chamberlains. They crossed the Great Hall and positioned themselves on both sides of the throne-platform. Again the gong sounded—once, twice....

A curtain opened and Maya appeared, followed by her ladies in waiting. Her slender figure was draped in white silk, her only adornment consisted of strings of pearls one of which had been woven through her shiny hair. She took her seat on the left of the two thrones. Her gaze began to travel through the Hall. She seemed satisfied, for she gave Premenio a friendly smile which he acknowledged with a bow.

The trumpets resounded from the towers, the gong rang out thrice—and Nabor entered, alone. Dark purple and silver, his favorite colors, adorned him: a silver head-band from which a large topaz was hanging down in front of his forehead, crowned his head. Topaz of all sizes flashed forth their yellowish fire from silver-plated necklaces and bracelets around his neck and arms, as well as from the silver trimmings of his robe. The Lucoman of

Mayagard wore silver shoes which sparkled softly as he crossed the Hall. The entire court bowed low as he passed. Maya had risen. The purple color all around him made Nabor's sharp-edged features appear even paler. But a tender smile smoothed the sharp lines of his face, as he offered the royal kiss to his wife. Moving with ease, he sat down beside her, signaling to Mamya, "Bring in the foreigner!" Accompanied by other officials Mamya left to fetch the Tursian prince. They reached his dwelling by a soft carpet-covered path along which numerous palace boys were posted with torches in their hands. And, eventually, led by Mamya and Eseko—and surrounded by the other officials who had come along—Wea was brought into the Great Hall. Confronted with the staggering splendor of the room, he stopped in surprise. He also wore a festive robe—a white dress strewn with rubies, a garment Maya had presented him with—which made his dark skin appear even darker, his black hair even blacker. He stepped up to the royal couple with smooth, singularly springy steps. Eseko stayed closely behind him in case of sudden difficulties in the mutual linguistic exchange.

Nabor's eyes traveled over Wea's person with astonishment. Like Maya before him, he also felt the exotic charm of the Tursian. He rose to his feet, bowed his head and said,

"Welcome, Wea, Prince of Tursia! We offer you our hospitality and the protection of our country. Your well-being and comfort will be our foremost concern."

Everybody present was not a little surprised when Wea answered Nabor's words with well-constructed sentences in the language of Eya-Eya and only slightly tainted by his Tursian accent. Maya looked gratefully at Eseko who smiled with satisfaction. The old man had invested much effort in teaching Wea the Atlanteans' tongue. Fortunately the Tursian's tenacity and power of attention had made his task easier. Nabor waved and Premenio came forward to guide Wea to a couch standing near the throne. Attendants were at the guest's service at once. Music could be heard as the festive evening—a symphony of beauty and splendor satisfying all the senses—began. Wea was only accompanied back to his apartment when the sun rose out of the sea in the early hours of the following morning.

Large herds of wild horses were roving through the flower-strewn meadows of Eya-Eya. They were easy to catch, as in Eya-Eya all animals lived harmoniously side by side and man had so far left them to prosper in peace. In Atlantis human beings played with the animals or used them for certain types of labor. A holy law forbade endangering the animals' lives. This was the reason why the Tursians' lawless hunting stunned the Mayas. With disgust they observed the aliens roast the flesh of the killed animals over open fires—and then eat it! Whenever Nabor drove through the countryside he heard heart-rending complaints: "They are scaring the animals, Sire. They've become frightened and jumpy, avoiding us; and when we follow them they turn against us."

For the first time Nabor realized how much depended on a guest's behavior—especially if it was an unbidden one. He began to ponder and to ruminate on how to meet this challenge. But he could not make up his mind. The rules of hospitality forbade him to send the strangers away. Besides, would they go if he asked them to? They had spears with shiny metal tips, weapons they hurled through the air in a deadly fashion. He knew they would not stop short at taking even human life. How powerless he actually was with all his wealth and magnificence! These aliens were sure to destroy the Atlanteans' pure consciousness!

"Help us, *Elohim*!" he prayed in his heart. "Take the dark burden from us!"

As he prayed thus, a gentle whiff like a breeze came floating around him, enveloping him, taking all heaviness away from him. Blissfully he closed his eyes. A bright glow blazed up inside him and as if transcending itself, his soul streamed away into that Light. The subtlest of voices whispered within him, "Wait for your hour to come!"

At that moment Maya entered. She saw her husband lying on his bed as if asleep, his face beautified by his distant smile. When she stepped closer, Nabor opened his eyes—and she saw a magical brilliance shine forth at her.

"You were asleep, my beloved," she said tenderly.

He got up and drew her to him. She started to play with his long curls.... He felt the warmth of her beautiful womanhood and his slender hands went over her lovingly.

"You are always so far away and so silent these days."

But Maya's words remained as if suspended in mid-air. Nabor's face had become grave. Maya continued, "Often I don't recognize you since you returned from inside Bayagard's walls." He heard her and, as his eyes traveled away into the distance, he moved away from her. For a while silence reigned between them—a silence in which Maya could hear her heart throb.... When his answer came at last it was spoken solemnly and his face appeared transfigured: "I was touched by *Elohim*'s Light."

Maya stared at him in surprise, her heart skipping a beat.

"It is Huatami speaking through his mouth!"—the idea hit her with paralyzing evidence. What she had feared most had come to pass. Without a word she reclined in his arms for a short moment, then—managing a smile—she freed herself. She knew she must be alone now. It was indeed a bitter realization that from now on she would have to share her dearest with the one she hated the most.

Meanwhile, Nabor—enraptured by the bliss of his state of consciousness—was not unaware of the transformation in Maya. Again he drew her close but she freed herself reluctantly. There was a new coldness about her, a new hard glint in her eyes. "Wea has asked us to go hunting with him," she said coldly.

"Hunting?" Nabor said perplexed; and he continued, "May that bloody custom of those foreigners be spared us!"

Provoked by the firm tone of this statement, Maya said, "A man's courage is steeled in danger."

"There is no courage in murdering a defenseless animal," Nabor replied quietly.

"The Atlanteans avoid fighting because they are afraid!" Maya replied in defiance.

"What are you talking about, Maya!" Nabor exclaimed, aghast.

But by now Maya could not hold back any longer. Her eyes shone with blazing fury; agonizing bitterness within made her burst out in anger, "You Atlanteans are but cowards at heart! Under the spell of your priests—that's what you are! They make the laws that bind your hands. They order you about like little children. You are not masters of yourselves but slaves to *their* will! They broke *even your* proud, freedom-loving mind, Nabor, shrouding your senses—and your heart!—in darkness!"

The Lucoman drew a deep breath. As if in self-defense, Nabor raised his hands. He was filled with sadness—and looked at his wife with compassion. Suddenly a gong was heard and a chamberlain entered almost at once. He said, "The Tursian prince is in the Great Hall."

"Maya," Nabor said with soft kindness, "let's explain to him that it is not customary for the nobility of Eya-Eya to scare the deer."

"I would have thought it a better custom to comply with a guest's wishes!" Maya replied, turning proudly to leave; a short movement of the closing curtain—and Nabor was alone.

For a while he walked the floor—then he stopped. All was clear to him now: If Maya, in her defiance, wanted to follow the foreigners in their ways—it was up to her! But he, Nabor, would remain faithful to himself and *Elohim*.

Wea was waiting with some of the captains of his tribe in the Great Hall. Dressed in his deer-skin garb and adorned with strings of animal horns, he walked the floor nervously. At last Maya arrived. She was clad in a long gown leaving her feet uncovered and her hair was held tightly in place by ribbons, a Tursian dagger hung from her belt. Wea expressed his admiration; she thanked him with a few brief words and looked around: Nabor had not yet arrived. She wondered what he had finally decided. Her inner anger had subsided but there was still an indefinable feeling of lingering uneasiness.

Mamya entered the Hall and approached with measured steps. "Where is the Lucoman?" Maya asked. Instead of answering,

Mamya turned to Wea and said "The Lucoman sends his thanks for your invitation but he—as is the rule of this country—considers it an impossible thing to go against the ethic standards of his ancestors...and wishes you luck in all your undertakings!"

The Tursian's dark eyes flashed at Maya in surprise, but she remained silent and kept her lips pressed shut; her eyes were but thin slits. So, Nabor was returning the ball to her? So, she had made him aware of the contradictory feelings in his heart? So, she had forced him to face the necessity to decide between following the dictates of his faith and obeying the rules of external honor as a host! But she also realized that she, too, had been maneuvered into a position where she must take a stance. To follow the Tursian prince would mean violating an unwritten law and taking sides with the foreigner against Nabor and her people, whereas to refuse the Tursian's invitation—as Nabor had done—would signal, to the foreigner, her submission and her yielding of her claim to power. Suddenly, seeing that she had been caught in her own net, Maya fell victim to a wild inner struggle. Minutes passed during which nobody moved, then Wea said; "Is the Queen not—here in her own country—master of her decisions?"

This remark turned the scale; Maya's pride flared up rebelliously—and with her head held high she preceded the Tursian chief out of the Hall. Wea smiled triumphantly; he desired this beautiful woman passionately, wanted to take her and possess her, if necessary by force....

Black stallions with white manes and tails—a rare achievement of Atlantean horse breeding—transported the light, two-wheeled carriage in a wild race through the streets of Mayagard out into the open country. The speed of the ride almost took Maya's breath away and her hands clasped the carriage's rim in a seizure of fright. But the charioteer's strong fists held the reins firmly and forced the spirited horses to comply with his will. Wea and his Tursian entourage came racing along behind the Queen's team-of-four. The Tursian riders were bent forward over the neck of their horses; they rode their mounts without a saddle or blanket, spurring them on with wild cries.

Nabor's eyes followed the hunting party from the roof of the Palace. There was a great emptiness within him and from time to time his throat felt so tight he thought he was being strangled. "Your path will be difficult," Huatami had said.

Although the sun was hot, the Lucoman experienced chills and when Mamya stepped onto the roof, Nabor's eyes met his with a blind stare. "He does not see me," Mamya thought, feeling a pang of compassion for the young ruler. He withdrew silently with a deep bow.

The hunting party's train was racing through the streets of the city with a roar. The Mayans looked up in surprise and not a few disapproving comments were heard, but in the intoxicating atmosphere of speed the Lucoman remained unaware of these things. Speeding along at such high velocity was like leaving all earthly gravity behind, like being seized by a rush of blissful freedom.

When the hunting grounds were reached, her carriage drove to the top of a small hill from which one had a fine view over vast meadows intermittently covered with low shrubbery and of many glittering brooks making their way through the green land, interspersed with rice paddies and stretching down toward the dark, distant forests.

In Eya-Eya the rice production was operated on a large scale, since—besides fruit—steamed rice constituted the most important element of Atlantean nutrition; all pastry and bread was made from rice flour. A mixture of milk, sugar and rice flour permitted the preparation of the most delicious dishes. Given the even, warm climate, the Atlanteans were partial to cold dishes. They also ate their steamed rice cold and chilled grape-juice or wine were their favorite drinks.

The hunting Tursians began fanning out across the countryside. Having formed a long line, they moved forward at first, then wheeled in one by one and—chasing through the meadows with loud clamor—they surrounded the frightened animals. Some of these were quickly killed by well-aimed spears, but suddenly a huge black panther emerged from the undergrowth and set out in powerful leaps toward the hill from which Maya, standing in her carriage, was observing the hunt. A group of Tursians were coming after the beast which—having been hit in the side by a spear—howled in pain. The brunt of the spear's thrust made the panther fall but soon he got back on his feet with a mighty bound, bawling loudly. The spear slipped from its wound and the cat continued up the hill. Unable to utter a sound, Maya stared into the bloodshot eyed of the enraged beast in terror. When the panther saw Maya, it briefly hesitated then crouched down, ready to jump. A piercing shriek from Maya—a dark figure leapt in front of her carriage—the flash of a dagger—and the animal collapsed with a gurgling cry as the weapon penetrated deep between its jaws.

The moment Wea had realized the danger of the situation, with the wounded panther starting up the hill on which he knew Maya to be, he had jerked his horse around and—standing on its back—had come over from the side of the hill at full speed. By making a powerful jump at the last moment, he had succeeded in averting the catastrophe.

Leaning against the rim of the carriage, Maya, as pale as death, thanked the prince with a faint smile. Some fresh water was hastily brought to her in a horn and she recovered her strength. It was only then that she realized that Wea's right hand was bleeding. In his agony the panther had dug his teeth deep into his arm. Wea fended off her worried questions with a smile; he agreed, however, to have some large leaves wrapped around his hand—then Maya gave the signal for the return home. Wea rode beside the horses of Maya's carriage in silence; he ordered the team to move in a slow gait, the deadly danger the Lucoman had just been in was still lingering with her. She glanced furtively at her rescuer.

What she saw was the very image of handsome manliness: Wea sat on his white horse as if it had been bred just to fit his body. His tawny face, his dashing profile and blue-black shiny hair, his muscular arms and legs—all of these conveyed the impression of self-confidence and power,

"I am still deeply moved by the courage, Wea, with which you rescued me from such great danger," Maya said admiringly. Gravely the Tursian replied, "My life is like a battle, my Queen! In the mountains and forests of my homeland, death is lurking in many different forms and only the experienced fighter will survive. The Tursians' life is hard indeed!"

"An Atlantean would never have done what you did," Maya said as if the thought had only now struck her.

"Your people, Milady, live in a beautiful dream. Never before had I laid eyes on such a magnificent country—a country where animals abound and fruits are found in such luxurious quantity and where man's life flows along without any hardship."

"Everything is just a game for them," the Lucoman replied bitterly. "They avoid all confrontation—and like sheep, they follow the shepherd, they obey their priests' commands—priests who promise them an even more blissful existence in *Elohim*'s Kingdom."

Wea looked at her inquisitively. Maya's words and tone of speech were a clear indication that the beautiful Queen was not happy. He replied cautiously, "I know nothing about *Elohim* and His Kingdom. As far as I'm concerned, it is the Sun God's Light and Glory that gives power and strength to our lives. His Being is all-permeating, he provides food for our body and his warmth cheers our hearts."

"The Sun God!" said Maya, trying to grasp the meaning of the word. "You mean the sun shining in the sky? How can it be a god?"

"Doesn't the sun awaken life in numerous forms and doesn't it make these awakened forms attain a wonderful perfection? Isn't there darkness and death where its rays don't reach?" Wea pointed out.

There was a short silence, then the Tursian added, "Again and again the sun rises victoriously, overcoming darkness' might. It rises and sets—and rises again. All life perceivable with our senses does likewise, my Queen!"

Maya was lost in her thoughts, Wea's words echoing in her mind. "How simple and natural this idea is," she finally agreed. "Your god stands before you clearly visible for your eyes; there is no dark secret shrouding him from your perception; he is a god kindly inclined toward this life—a god forever becoming, forever dying, a god close to man and directly observable in his powerful effects—whereas the God of Atlantis is a God in the dark; nobody knows Him, nobody has ever seen Him—only the priests speak of Him as if they knew...."

"Anything your senses cannot perceive, my Queen, is but a dream," Wea said firmly. Then he added, "My god is the god of action. He is a warrior. He fights and is victorious—and human beings must fight like him if they want to exist. The victorious ones are close to him, not the priests whose only task it is to praise him. This is why the priests are the warriors' servants and helpers."

Maya's eyes widened. What she heard was like a wonderful tale to her ears.

"If ever I am granted a son, I want the Sun's freedom to be about him. I want him to look for dangerous situations like a warrior and to master danger like a warrior. I want him to be his own master—and not a servant to the priesthood!" she exclaimed, her green eyes flashing with determination and her voice at a metallic pitch.

The sight of Maya in her excitement, the sight of this woman more beautiful than any other he had ever seen, all but took Wea's breath away. Filled with an unmitigated desire to make her his own, he bent forward and held out his right hand. "This hand which protected you from danger is also laying an empire at your feet—an empire where you would be queen after your own taste. Any priest or servant foolhardy enough to resist you, the Queen, would be smashed by this fist like a dog!"

This violent outburst on the part of the otherwise so self-possessed Tursian prince aroused the most contradictory feelings in Maya. With her mouth shut tightly, her lips thin and tense, her features non-committal and her eyes hidden behind long silky eye-lashes, the Lucoman drove through the busy streets of Mayagard in silence and unmoving like a statue.

When they arrived at the Palace and Wea helped her down from the carriage, her gaze penetrated his and she said with a smile, cautiously touching his wounded right hand, "I owe my life to this hand—and it is this hand I shall call upon when the time comes for my freedom-loving heart to break out of the present narrowness of my life."

"I shall be waiting, Milady, just as the Tursian Empire is waiting for its Queen." Wea's dark eyes shone with joy. He felt a violent urge to pull her to him but—controlling himself—he simply bowed down somewhat ceremoniously but full of dignity. Then—as required by etiquette—he gave way for her to pass.

Maya's feet felt heavy when she climbed up the steps to the Palace. How should she face her husband? She thrust back her head haughtily and straightened up with pride. She would fight for her interests and for her son's freedom! With this resolve she stepped through the gate, upright. To her surprise, Nabor's welcome was friendly. She had expected reproaches and had already armed herself mentally, but nothing of the sort was forthcoming. The Lucoman was as calm as ever—only in his distant eyes she thought she could detect a lingering sadness. To hide her uneasiness, Maya began to relate her adventure and praised the Tursian's courageous exploit by which he had rescued her from deadly danger. Nabor listened in silence, then he said, "I'll reward him royally, of course, for his heroic deed."

"You'd only hurt his feelings a second time—for you did so already by not accepting his invitation to the hunt," Maya replied angrily.

"You must be tired, Maya, and should get some rest," was his quiet answer. Then, turning away from her, he left the Hall: "I must go and see Wea at once," he thought.

Confronted with her husband's even temperament, Maya's resolve lost its vigor and she began to feel forlorn. "He just makes light of me, treating me like a stubborn child," she thought bitterly. An invisible barrier seemed to have been erected between them.

"There is still time for me to go back—but at what cost!" she thought. Once more the events of the last few hours came back to her down to the minutest detail. Wea's image rose up before her mental eye. He certainly desired her! She had suspected as much for a long time, but today that suspicion had become a certainty. Wea or Nabor? The first, in the full bloom of his manhood and deeply involved in life: a barbarian certainly, but capable of true self-transformation; the second, descendant of an ancient royal dynasty, refined down to his toes and a perfect example of Atlantean mentality and culture—a man with no ambition other than to live his life in harmony and beauty before returning, eventually—after having attained freedom from all dark shadows—to the very Kingdom of Light his devoted heart believed in.

Maya's breathing became difficult as she realized she would not be able follow Nabor on his path! She loved the throb of life, she loved power and movement, she wanted to rule and make decisions according to her own discretion. She had hoped to do so through him but that hope had been broken. He simply—albeit kindly—put her in her place—the place of a wife, and took away her power, leaving it to her to resign herself to the facts. At that moment Maya did not know what to make of it all; she felt uprooted, wondering who might be able to help her. The God of Atlantis only helped those who submitted to His priests, but she, Maya, did not trust those priests, she had become a stranger in their world, the world she had been born into! Again Wea's dashing features appeared before her. "The Tursian Empire is awaiting its Queen...." She could still hear his words. And suddenly a triumphant smile illuminated her beautiful face—a smile, however, with a hard brilliance to it.

Eseko was very surprised to suddenly find the Lucoman standing in the hall of the building which accommodated the Tursian chief. The old steward greeted his king with much ceremony and bows but Nabor's eye went beyond him; he paid no attention to the fine-sounding phrases and laconically asked to see Wea.

"He has already withdrawn for the night, Sire. His hand was bleeding from the wound caused by the panther's bite. I took care of his injury—and now he is asleep," the old man remarked obsequiously.

"Tell him I'm here waiting for him," Nabor said calmly. Eseko hurried away. While the Lucoman was waiting, he turned his senses inward, for he knew—the final decision was due—here and now.

After Maya had left him, he had spent long hours struggling for inner composure in fervent prayers on the battlements of his palace. The pain that had followed the initial emptiness had been so lacerating that he had felt like being torn asunder by a storm. Eventually, however, his woeful heart had recovered its courage with his lips stammering in a whisper, "If it is your will, *Elohim*, then so be it!"—and, peace had returned to him. In this newly found silence he again had heard that subtlest of murmurs, "The sacrifice of your heart will free Atlantis from the horde of the Dark Ones. Let them go in peace—and your wife too, as she loves herself more than she loves you." At this his humble heart had trembled in a last agonizing flutter, and then he had endorsed his fate with a level mind.

The sound of clanking weapons made him turn his head. Wea had entered the hall. The Tursian prince stood before him, a heavy breastplate of small metal leaves encasing his shoulders and chest. Nabor thanked him politely for Maya's rescue. The Tursian parried with evident pride, "It was my duty to save the Queen, since it was I who had exposed her to danger."

Nabor nodded in agreement; then—on a sudden impulse—he went straight to the point: "The Tursian Empire has been without the guiding hand of its master for many months now. I almost feel guilty for keeping you away from your princely duties by having you as my guest here with me for so long." Wea was unable to hide the shock of his surprise and could not answer at once. An even-flowing cone of Light streaming forth from Nabor's eyes had enveloped him; at the same time a singular luminous glow could be seen around the Lucoman. The silent struggle between the two men lasted several seconds, then—unable to meet Nabor's stare any longer—the

Tursian's self-assurance wavered and he lowered his eyes to the ground.

"I had set out for conquest but your wife's beauty held me a prisoner, so I stayed on as her guest and kept my men's weapons checked through peaceful hunting."

"To fulfill your men's desires, all my men will help fill your ship with gold and precious stones—thus ensuring that your voyage was not in vain."

Indignation showed in Wea's face but he controlled his temper. "Your friendship's grace is riches enough for me to take home; I don't need your gold," he replied proudly.

"My friendship will be with you throughout your way back," Nabor said proffering his hand to the prince. Wea hesitated: would it be right to accept the friendship of a man whose wife he desired with all his senses? But then—had not the Atlantean dealt shrewdly with him, too? Thus, it would be shrewdness for shrewdness! And with his face twisting into a broad smile, he shook hands with the Lucoman. Nabor was aware of the Tursian's duplicity with painful clarity, but even if he had not sensed it, the cold stare of those black eyes wouldn't have left a doubt in him.

"Should I ever be granted the favor by the powers of fate to welcome you as a guest in our Tursian mountains, I shall certainly return your friendship," Wea resumed. "I cannot do so here. I have seen many things in your kingdom that seemed strange, others that could help to ease the Tursians' hard life."

"So chose yourself what you consider worthy of your interest, since neither gold nor precious stones are what you crave," Nabor said quietly, adding, "Eseko will be at your disposal to take down your wishes; it is his office to serve you."

"Your generosity shall be my guiding principle. My hand will only take what I regard as the most precious to take back to my forebears' land. Your words encourage the hope that my choice will not soil the days of our friendship." Wea's disdainful glance clearly underlined the treachery of his tongue. Nabor was profoundly nauseated by the moment's veiled hostility, but he saw no way to relieve it; he had simply done what had been asked of him. With this thought in mind he said. "Grant me the pleasure of entertaining you, my friend and guest, with a feast and with games before we have to part for a long time." His words were polite and so was the answer he received. "I shall be pleased to accept your invitation, as it is certainly a great honor to have been the friend of the Lucoman and a guest in his palace; but allow me to chose the hour myself."

"So be it, Prince! When you have made up your mind about the time of your departure, let me know!" Nabor said concluding their conversation, and—nodding briefly—he turned to leave. He was pale, the sides of his nose quivered. The contempt on the part of the Tursian chief—who surely thought he had won the game—almost over-taxed the strength of his self-control. Clearly the decision was with Maya now. If her heart had turned away from him then everything would happen in the sense of the revelation he had received by the subtle inner voice.

When he had recovered his composure he went to Maya's apartment. His grave, pale features startled her. Anticipating disaster, she asked, "How did you find Wea? Are his injuries a threat his life?"

"His wound seems to be harmless; the prince is well. On the other hand, he is thinking about returning to the land of his ancestors."

Slowly Nabor's words sank into Maya's restless soul. She mastered her inner turmoil with difficulty. Wea wanted to go home! The very thought of it felt like fire in her brain; she knew fate was asking for a final decision from her. Uncertain in her heart, she let her eyes roam nervously about the room.

"I left the choice to him as to what he'd take home with him. At any rate, he seems to be scorning gold and precious stones," Nabor informed her.

"You left the choice to him?" She looked at him in disbelief.

Nabor nodded. "That's right. He promised to take only what he considers the most precious goods in this country."

"The most precious goods?" A shock went through Maya. She scrutinized Nabor's face. Wasn't he even guessing what he had promised the Prince? But she found no answer in his self-possessed features. Finally Nabor said in a friendly tone, "The shadow that was caste over our destiny is receding; the days of happiness will come back to us...if your heart is willing."

Avoiding his eyes, Maya remained silent. He walked up to her. "Maya," he said lovingly. "Maya, for our own sake as well as the sake of our children, let's proceed to the end of the road together." He took her hand—but she turned away from him.

"The shadow you are talking about is only upon you; you have distanced yourself from me," she said feverishly. "How many times did I see you looking as if sunken away in a dream, although you were clearly wide awake; you were alive but you looked as if dead. That was not the Nabor to whom my heart had once gone out! Since your stay at Bayagard you have adopted the priests' unmanly ways. How can a priest be the ruler of a kingdom? It was I who checked the alien threat! It was I who forced the Tursian chief to go easy on his belligerent intentions. None of your priests helped you in this political dilemma! I stood alone—and I am still alone in this, for you have fallen victim to the priesthood's spell!"

Nabor remained silent and motionless. He heard the sound of her words—and yet he did not hear her. All he knew was that there was bitter, painful clarity in him. But his calm made her wrath break forth with unbridled violence: "Never, do you hear Nabor, Lucoman of my father's kingdom, never will I allow my son—whose face appeared to me in a dream—to become a nerveless tool in the priesthood's hands!"

Nabor bowed down and—without a word—went out of the room. This silent response was worse than any furious counter charge; in her helpless anger Maya pressed her fists to her mouth. A groan escaped her. So! He had released her! She meant that little to him! He did not even consider her worthy of an answer. What, then, was she to them all here? To whom did she mean anything, to whom was she important? Nobody understood her—apart from the alien! "The Empire of the Tursians is waiting for a queen," rang through her mind.

Tense and almost dismal, Maya felt a fateful decision ripening within her....

Assisted by Eseko, Wea was looking for and selecting such special items as he thought could be of use to his men and country. He was shown the various industries and crafts; he saw how the silk was rolled off the cocoon of the silk worm and spun into a thread, how skilled hands processed dyed silk into robes and coats and how these were decorated with silver and gold threads woven into the fabric, or embellished with trimmings, broad borders and belts encrusted with topaz, rubies, sapphires, emeralds, amethysts, or aquamarines of different shapes and sizes. He witnessed goldsmiths shaping gold and silver rings and bracelets and decorating them with various gems. Anklets were also made to sparkle with precious stones of many different colors. The Tursian was virtually blinded by the glittering objects he saw. The prodigious abundance of precious trinkets and the beauty of their forms and shapes enthralled him; the unending wonders of craftsmanship displayed before him thoroughly aroused his enthusiasm.

Eseko also took him to the gigantic marble quarries, to the masons and sculptors working the stone. Everywhere he went, the Tursian's eyes met with the same outstanding combination of artisan skill and artistic taste that only a people of high cultural standards could have produced.

One day passed and then one night. Nabor, the Mayan ruler, found himself engaged in a strenuous inner struggle. For him, Maya was the very image of all the beauty of this world. His love for her—by which the totality of his being had been subtly permeated—had been laid about her like a precious coat and Maya herself had been moved by the power of his feelings to respond in kind. At first defiant, willfulness had sometimes flared up inside her but gradually he had—or so, at least, he thought—chased away such dark clouds. Now, however, it seemed that the overwhelming desire for power in the Lucoman had only been suppressed and had returned now, entirely permeating her soul.

His dream of happiness had been shattered. Maya had become a stranger to him—a stranger uttering loud reproaches against him. But her son—his son!—who will be born as her dream had shown her, that son in whose person he wished to perfect himself—that son, who was to become the ruler of the kingdom when he, Nabor, had returned to *Elohim*'s Realm, his son, then, was an Atlantean—and was to remain an Atlantean! Would it be possible for him to force her to wait until the child entered the earthly plane? Into this inner debate of his own thoughts the mysterious "voice" broke—at first hardly audible, then clearly intelligibly with the words, "Do as you are told!"

Deep silence reigned within him. Then he thought, "I am going to give way. The Lucoman shall not be forced to steal away in the dark of the night. She is mistress of her own destiny and she must be permitted to leave in freedom—if she so wishes."

Nabor went over to one of the marble tables on which a golden dish was set and which held a golden ball that he sent whirring with a circular movement of his hand. The sound called in a servant.

"Fetch Mamya, the Steward!" Nabor ordered.

Mamya came swiftly—and was taken aback by Nabor's appearance: the Lucoman seemed to have aged by years! Nevertheless, his face remained impenetrable when he spoke.

"Fit out the big barque; I want to use it for a long voyage along the coast. Tell Milady that when the sun sinks for the third time the towers of Mayagard will greet me again. Until then, everything will be under her command." The Lucoman fell silent, adding after some time, "Only Ekloh is to accompany me."

⁂

Maya steered her team-o-four through the bustling streets of the capital. She had to get out! The Palace's thick walls oppressed her; she wanted to see people—lots of people—to distract her from her inner unrest. When she passed the large house of the sculptor Remalya, she noticed a great number of carriages collecting in front of the building and the horses of these carriages were held by Tursians. She turned to the charioteer behind her in surprise and asked, "Who is blocking the road there?"

"The foreign prince is with Remalya. They say that Remalya is making a statue of him" was the reply.

Maya registered this information incredulously, for there was an unwritten law in Eya-Eya that only the twelve noble ancestors should be portrayed, and no Atlantean would be presumptuous enough to disregard that law. The Lucoman stepped down from her carriage and, led by servants, went into Remalya's work-shop. Immersed in his work, the sculptor was modeling Wea's head in clay. The Tursian sat in an armchair not far away from him. Seeing Maya, he stood up in surprise; joy shone in his eyes. Also Remalya had quickly turned around and was now bowing deeply.

"It's not customary in the kingdoms of Atlantis to make a sculptured likeness of human beings," Maya said coolly.

Confounded, the sculptor assured her that he was only doing what the foreigner had asked him—but one motion of Maya's hand ordered him to be silent. She closely inspected the sculpture. What she saw was Wea's bold face smiling at her. "Destroy it!" she ordered laconically, turning to the artist.

Startled, Remalya looked at Wea, but one indignant motion of Maya's hand—and he obeyed her order. Wea intervened by saying provocatively, "It is not customary in Tursia to insult a guest by ignoring his wishes."

Maya looked at him: "Even if the Queen gives the order to do so?"

"The guest's desire is regarded of greater importance than a queen's command," Wea replied proudly.

"There is a law in Eya-Eya…," Maya began in a conciliatory tone, but Wea interrupted her, "Did you not say, Milady, that the laws in this country are the laws made by its priests?"

Maya felt silent. He was right. So she asked more amicably, "Who gives the Tursians their laws?"

"During the holy 'thing' the chieftains and the free men decide on everything; life and death of their men depend on these decisions."

"And they don't take the priests' advice?"

"The holy duty of the priests consists solely in serving the godhead, in studying the course of the stars and in revealing the meaning that this course will have for us humans." Then he added, "The priest also bows to the warlord, who protects the holy shrine with his sword."

Remalya served them wine in golden cups. Wea emptied his in one gulp, whereas Maya only sipped once. Wea resumed his explanations by saying, "There is one question I am burning to ask you—but this is neither the time nor place to do so, Milady." A clear sound of wooing permeated his words and the fire in his eyes betrayed his all-encompassing desire. The Lucoman felt attracted to the Tursian but she also shrank from his forward ways. She had never seen sensual hunger in Nabor's eyes; her husband's glance had always shone with loving kindness only. Instinctively she realized that when two souls are eager to unite, they meet in chastity and mutual respect. The bond of marriage was holy to the Atlanteans and never would an Atlantean man have approached the wife of another. Maya looked at Wea with unflinching directness, thinking that she would not mind taming this 'black panther', as she secretly called him. With a superior smile on her lips she said, "If I were the Queen of the Tursians, my will would be law!" Wea gazed at this beautiful, regal woman, knowing that he desired her with all his senses. And her words gave him reason to hope. He seized her hand impulsively and said with sparkling eyes, "And it would be my law to serve the Queen...."

Withdrawing her hand, the Lucoman took one step away from him. "I shall remember your words, should I ever require your services," she replied—and quickly turned to leave.

Wea followed her out of the building and accompanied her to the Lucoman's Palace. There, Maya—crossing the Hall—went directly to her apartment. Her ladies in waiting started fussing about her at once. Milady was clearly in high spirits—indeed, she even jested with her maids!

When Mamya, the Steward, entered the room just then, his distinctly solemn demeanor caused the Lucoman burst out into happy laughter. She called to her ladies, "Off with you, you jolly little birds, the mighty Steward of the Palace has arrived with some utterly urgent information!"

Mamya forced a smile, but almost at once his face resumed a deeply serious expression. Maya began to have misgivings; something unusual must have occurred. And indeed—somewhat hesitatingly yet in a clear voice the Steward reported that the Lucoman had left on the royal barque.

"What—Nabor's taken to sea?"

After the first surprised shock Maya understood: he had put all ruling power into her hands for three days! Free from all fettering influence that his physical presence might bring to bear on her, she was to gain clarity alone as to what to decide. He did not fight for her—he simply left her to her own devices.

Silence reigned in the room. Mamya did not dare to speak up. He was guessing more than he actually knew, but he had feared this development would come to pass. He had always been aware of Maya's touchy pride; often enough he had had to wrestle with her after her father's death to prevent her from engaging in some unreasonable course of action. But now genuinely shattering circumstances had come into play—circumstances he did not have the courage to spell out even to himself!

Morose and withdrawn, the Lucoman sat brooding gloomily. Then suddenly she was on her feet and, straightening herself up, she ordered in a brash, unfamiliar voice, "Fetch the Tursian prince!"

Mamya turned pale and raised his arms as if in self-defense, but the green-shimmering eyes of the Queen were flashing forth at him, when she said, "Did you not hear my orders?"—and the Steward, recoiling, chose to withdraw without a comment. He returned with Wea only a short time later. The prince was dressed in Atlantean fashion.

"You called me, Milady, so I came at once to learn your desire!" he said, looking at Maya with anticipation.

The Lucoman motioned to Mamya to leave, then she turned to Wea:

"Sooner than I expected, Prince, do I require a friend's helping hand!"

Her words came slowly, rich in emphasis and her gaze was fully on him. Wea's response was unbridled joy. "My Queen!" he cried out enraptured. The thought that he had, so quickly, come this close to his goal intoxicated him. "Just tell me what I must do! I'll do anything for you!"—and it was only Maya's continued formal bearing which induced him to retain his sobriety.

"Anything? Anything, Prince?" she asked with cool deliberation.

"Anything, my Queen!" he repeated, holding out his right hand.

"In that case, listen! For the sake of my son whom I want to be a free man, I am ready to go to the Tursian kingdom with you."

"My Queen!" Wea interjected exultantly.

A haughty smile briefly went over Maya's features—then she proceeded: "You promised to serve the Queen and now the Queen has decided to follow you as your guest. Don't ever forget that—or else I'll leave you!"

Disappointment showed all over Wea's face, yet—mechanically—he nodded agreement.

"You have my word, Milady," he replied in a low voice. Then, pulling himself together, he added, "No Tursian nobleman has ever broken his word!"

"Then wait for me at the third sunset!" she said and it sounded to him like an order. He seemed abashed—so, relenting, Maya assured him of her pleasure at being granted the opportunity to see his kingdom.

According to the directions given by the Lucoman, everything was made ready for the great voyage. Meanwhile, she herself was wandering through the Palace, bidding farewell to all the familiar rooms. Here she had been a happy child, protected by a gentle father who had always let her have her way in an attempt to make up for the loss of the little girl's mother who had died giving birth to the child. The father had brought up the girl like a boy, had her accompany him on his travels and given her all possible opportunities to live out the days of her youth to the fullest. After this happy childhood, luck seemed to have smiled on the princess once more the day she had been given the blond son of the Bor dynasty for a husband: but all that was over and finished now, she thought, a shadow moving over her countenance. Sadness was about to engulf her but she shook her head indignantly to rid herself of the depressing mood.

It was a magnificent procession when the Lucoman—clad in the shiny azure-blue royal coat and preceded by all the stewards and attendants of the Palace, all the chamberlains and ladies in waiting, walked through the lane of palace boys and servants toward Wea's vessel, waiting to take her away to a far and foreign land. The population of Mayagard had gathered to do homage to its Queen and greeted her in silence. The trumpets' sound rang out into the distance, but there was not a single stir of joy in the crowd. They all realized that something incomprehensible was happening right there before their eyes—for who had ever seen a Lucoman leaving her kingdom, a wife abandoning her husband—the man she had been bound to in a holy ceremony? Only the foreigners were rejoicing. Their chief stood proudly displaying a triumphant smile and awaiting the Queen on his ship. As for Maya herself, her heart was weary. There was a suffocating sensation in her throat but she fought the painful feeling with cold pride. When she stepped on board, she heard Wea utter a well-worded speech but she could only smile unhappily when she took his hand and was helped across the large plank leading to the ship. Almost at once the vessel detached itself from the shore, the oars started to move rhythmically—and the entire fleet veered toward the open sea.

From an elevated seat Maya saw her homeland disappear in the distance. No emotions showed on her face. Inside she felt nothing but emptiness: there she was, traveling toward an unknown fate—without desire, without joy.

Those who had come to see her off, slowly returned to their homes and the Palace. Only Premenio, walking between Mamya and Eseko, couldn't help break the silence. "What is our Master going to say when he comes back?" he exclaimed.

Mamya shrug his shoulders; only the aged Eseko did not care to hide his anger. He said "The Lucoman is giving herself into the hands of these savages. Our Master will never approve of this. He knows that the people of Eya-Eya are the chosen people of *Elohim* and that it is *Elohim*'s will that we keep clear of the Dark Ones."

The Tursian fleet left the canal. The broad sails were raised and immediately caught by the wind with crackling sounds as the ships made their way swiftly along the coast. After they had sailed for some time, a large barque was sighted coming toward them. It was white and golden and sparkling in the light of the setting sun. Its sail had been lowered and it was propelled forward by oarsmen. Soon Wea's ships were abreast with it and wild howling broke out on the Tursian decks, a frenzied calling—which, however, remained unanswered. On the prince's own vessel the barque had aroused interest: Wea himself—together with his officers—was watching the boat as if hypnotized and when the two vessels passed each other, his face assumed the expression of a bird of prey: over there, on a bed covered with precious silkspreads lay the proud Lucoman whose wife he was abducting. Maya turned her head from her elevated seat under a canopy. One glance—and she knew who—and what!—it was! Had not this royal barque of the Mayan rulers served her many times on her outings on the sea? She saw her husband too: There he was, reclining as if resting and perfectly relaxed, floating by and paying no heed to her at all. Only Ekloh, his Chamberlain, stood at the bow of the ship, looking across at her.

The day was drawing to a close and the coolness of the night soon enveloped her. Bedded in soft furs, the Lucoman lay dreaming. Only from time to time was she aware of foreign voices calling out. But eventually, the murmuring waves cradled her into sleep.

Anchored in the shallow water, the white royal barque lay gently rocking in a small creek hidden within the cliffs. Its golden embellishments were shining in the sunlight and its oars hung leisurely on either side of the ship's hull; it's sail was lowered. Everything on board seemed lifeless and nobody was to be seen on deck. At a short distance and on a narrow beach, some oarsmen and palace attendants were busy putting up small tents made of carpets for the night. Laughing and chatting happily they went about their work. Ekloh, the royal chamberlain, had informed them that they were to stay here for a few days. Some of the boys threw off their clothes and ran off into the water; swimming across the creek they reached the open sea.

Now Ekloh himself—walking with a dignified, measured step—could be seen approaching from the ship. Having come up to the tents, he called out in a hushed tone, "Keep quiet so that your clamor does not disturb our Master!"

The cheerful little crowd fell silent at once. What might have happened for their good Master to set out so suddenly for this voyage into the solitude by the seashore? Nobody ever saw him—only the chamberlain was allowed near him. Could he be ill? He had not been looking at all well recently.

In the meantime the Lucoman was lying as if dead upon his silk-covered bed under a tapestried canopy. His pale face was emaciated and looked much older, his closed eyes were set deeply in their sockets. Ekloh had cautiously stepped closer in the early hours after the first night. When he saw his Master in this condition, it struck him like a shock: Was the Lucoman dead? But bending over him, he realized that Nabor was breathing—so, the chamberlain withdrew quietly.

As for Nabor himself, only after a serious effort had he succeeded in quieting down the emotional storm within. Again and again Maya's beloved image had appeared before his soul's eye. The absolute sweetness of his desire for her consolidated in images that kept caressing his senses and would not let go of him. There were voices whispering inside of him to suggest he start making use of the hidden powers he had gained: it was easy to subjugate an unsettled soul, to take it into bondage—but Nabor also sensed the icy touch of the dark powers' presence—he even *saw* dark, wide-eyed faces crowding in front of his inner Light in an attempt to obscure it with their black shadow. But just as he was struggling to free himself from these visions and to turn toward the Light, gray-shadowy arms reached out for him. He distinctly felt being seized roughly and imperiously by those shadowy hands. Fear invaded him; he wanted to shake off the touch of those fingers—but could not. Something heavy had come to lie on him with paralyzing pressure and was breathing an icy blast at him. In his distress he cried out loud, calling the name of his beloved teacher into the mild night: "Tenupo! Tenupo—help!"

Seconds passed, each one seeming like an eternity. Then, suddenly, a beam of light flashed up in the far distance and began moving toward him and enveloping him: In this light he saw the kind face of the one he had called. Hands shining with light blessed him—and the Dark Ones disappeared; the heavy pressure lifted from him—only an inexpressible sensation of bliss remained to occupy his suffering being. He abandoned himself to the radiation of his helper like a happy child. In this inner oneness he was able to intuitively grasp Tenupo's thoughts: "Fear not, Nabor! The Helpers from the Light are forever ready to protect you when you call them. You were given great power—and an even greater power keeps you from harm wherever you go. Just follow your inner voice!"

As these words were spoken, he saw—in the light which enveloped him and as if in waves upon waves of magma—Tenupo's familiar face smiling at him with boundless kindness.

The day was fading and the night came with all its starry splendor. Again Nabor was transported into raptures. His soul had flown far away, and only his body was lying upon his regal bed. Once again the sun arose in the East—and once again it descended in the West. On the third day, just as it was reaching its zenith, the Lucoman began stirring. He rose to a sitting position and looked around in search of Ekloh, who soon appeared. Seeing that his Master was surrounded by a bright glow, he approached with reverence.

"Lift the anchor, we're going home!" Nabor's voice was as low as the humming of the breeze, as if afraid that something inexpressibly beautiful might be destroyed by its sound. He sank back into the cushions, his eyes closed and once again he drifted off into meditational absorption.

A vision rose before him in which he saw Mayagard, its Palace and the citizens walking hither and thither. They were carrying trunks to the Tursian ships. Huge crowds were gathering—crowds that kept moving closer to the port. A woman was turning her head. Maya! She seemed like a stranger and so serious! The fleet left the harbor.

She was gone....

He felt no pain; his mental eye saw nothing but blazing light; there was but holy, blissful silence within.

Shortly before they reached Mayagard, Nabor rose and called for his Chamberlain.

"Sire, the Tursians have gone. They sailed past us hours ago." Nabor nodded, "I know, Ekloh."

The Lucoman returned home. He found nothing but embarrassed faces around him. Hesitatingly Mamya began his report, but he had hardly uttered the first few words when a gesture from Nabor stopped him. The Lucoman greeted the court with complete calm, as if nothing had happened. Everything continued as before; the days passed in peaceful uniformity. Often the Lucoman showed himself in Mayagard's streets, leading his team-of-four through the thronging crowd with a sure hand while everybody stepped aside to make way for him. Only the children would flock around the chariot and he spoke to them often, taking some of them with him and then sending them home from the Palace with their arms full of presents. He also ventured often to the seashore, sat down on a high rock and listened to the lovely song of the waves. There, one day, the wish arose in him to live in a palace built high up on the cliffs, facing the limitless ocean. It would have to be a palace like a dream hewn in marble with terraces cascading down to the very sea. He immediately had Remalya and other artists come and listened to their suggestions. The project took shape quickly; many hands got busy to make the Lucoman's wish come true.

The "Palace of the Thousand Columns," as he people soon called it, soon rose up above the ocean like a vision of marble blossoms.

Winding columns supported upon their capitals—themselves richly embellished with flower motifs—loftily sweeping arches which by spreading out into a network of intertwining curved marble branches gave support to the high ceilings. Purple curtains hung from horizontal silver rods which connected the columns with one another. Heavy, closely set silver tassels adorned the upper edge of these silk curtains and silver braids ran along their lower rim. The carpets, couches as well as the seats of the chairs were all in purple and silver, artfully framed by white marble. Pillared colonnades, running down to the very edge of the ocean, crossed brightly gleaming white marble terraces at regular intervals along their way.

Most of the Lucoman's household had soon been transferred to the Palace of the Thousand Columns. Nabor was happy. There were no walls shutting him off from the world as all rooms and the large halls were formed exclusively by columns and curtains and, when he stepped out onto the terrace, he saw the sea stretching out before him in all its blue-green glory into what seemed to be a limitless distance. And at night, when lying on his bed, he heard the waves with a murmur tell stories of distant lands.

One day, he called for the young priest, Amatur. Immersed in deep conversation, they were soon walking through the rooms of the Palace, enjoying the beautiful vistas that opened up before them again and again. In his quiet and measured manner the young priest allowed himself to be carried along by the secret rhythm of this enchanting stroll.

"Do you know, Amatur, why all this came about?" Nabor asked with a sweeping movement of his arm.

"I can only guess, Lucoman," the priest replied, thinking of his ruler's destroyed marital happiness—but he said nothing about that. Nabor looked into the priest's eyes and the warmth he found there touched him and incited him to talk.

"Do you see the towers of the old Lucoman's Palace over there? I always felt like a stranger there, like no more than a guest—not to mention the terrible suffering I experienced within those walls. I fled from that suffocating, painful narrowness to the vast openness of the sea. As you may know, I stayed on the ocean for three days and three nights—and there, far away from all human influence, my soul was able to abandon itself to *Elohim*'s light. I struggled and grappled with dark powers who—because I was bound to the desires of the body—sought to confuse my mind. But I received help and was freed from suffering. Since that day I love the vastness of the sea more than ever. It was an inner vision which brought about this place—this house, where I can feel closely united with...her soul."

"When you returned from Bayagard, your eyes' brilliance gave me to understand that you had become a citizen of two worlds." He fell silent—then, with an imploring gesture of his hands, he added, "Grant me the favor of being your disciple, Enlightened One!"

"Not my disciple, Amatur," Nabor said warmly, while holding out his hand to the priest. "Let me call you 'friend'! We are, all of us, disciples of the sublime Beings of Light and nobody has the right to put himself above anyone else. On the other hand, a friend with whom I'd be united in the same endeavor would be a precious thing to have!"

"I take your hand with pleasure, Lucoman...!" the priest replied deeply moved, adding, "...and will serve you with all my being."

The two men stood hand in hand for some moments. It was like two souls greeting each other in the happiness of shining eyes.

"For you I am no longer the Lucoman—nor the Enlightened One! I am your friend Nabor and I am hoping—for my own benefit—to always remain your friend."

Engaged in a profound and meaningful conversation, the two friends were oblivious of time and place. Only when nightfall had come and the torches were lit did Amatur return to the Temple.

Once again it was the Night of Light. Nabor had traveled to Bayagard accompanied by Amatur and a large entourage and was greeted by his parents. His elder brother Sebor was also present. Sebor was as tall as a giant, topping all the other Lucoman and princes by a head's length. He informed his brother excitedly about a great number of projects that had aroused his interest, the realization of which had become especially important to him in his role as crown prince of Bayagard. However, he ended his exposition on a discouraged note, by saying, "But what's the use of planning and building if we must expect armed hordes of barbarians to enter our country one of these days! We should rather get ready to defend ourselves if we don't want to perish."

In the Council of Kings similar ideas were proposed. The events that had shaken the Mayan Kingdom gave rise to lively discussion. All the Lucoman were agreed that a recurrence of those events must be prevented. Nabor gave a description of the Tursian weapons and displayed a number of their spears and daggers. The steward Eseko was also called in to report on the production of these weapons, insofar as he had been able to become acquainted with the Tursian methods. Iron, the metal used for the manufacture of these weapons, was unknown in Atlantis. Hence, it was decided to find ferrous ores and to start the production of weapons on a large scale. Since the use of the weapons would require training, each of the kingdoms agreed to put its soldiers through such a course. Nobody mentioned Maya. By her decision to leave she had excluded herself from the Atlantean community and was considered dead. When the Lucoman had reached their decision about the introduction of iron weapons the resolution was submitted to the Loki. Huatami received them at the Temple to give his answer. He spoke clearly and deliberately. "Make it known to the peoples of Eya-Eya that each one of us must pray with more fervent devotion than ever before for the protection and safety of the Empire. When danger knocked at our door recently, one of us made a sacrificial offering as total as if he had given his very heart's blood—and it was this offering which stopped the danger." The Loki's eyes turned to Nabor who received the honor bestowed upon him by the Priest-King with his head bowed low. Huatami continued, "If all Atlanteans were like him, our ancestor's light-filled empire would arise again in new glory. O, you Lucoman, know and tell your people that the struggle against oneself is far more difficult than the struggle against another. He who wins the struggle against his own self does not need any weapons, for he generates powers that protect him wherever he goes. But those who wander through their days dreaming like children, who are reluctant to travel the narrow path toward the Light, those men and women are in no way different from the Dark Ones and we must fight them off using the same kind of weapons the Dark Ones use themselves. Learn to recognize *Elohim*'s signals! He wants to test His people. He wants to test each one of us! Those who let go of His hand must fight for their life, but woe be to those who start that fight with their mind's clarity obscured by the dark cloud of the thirst for power!" Huatami's ecstatic eyes were flashing like sudden flames and his tall emaciated figure stood very erect as he added these final words of gloomy prophesy: "If you are not satisfied with what you are, Atlanteans, the cold metal in your fist will turn into a weapon against yourselves and your children. When the greed for power flashes forth from a human being's eyes, this world may be gained, but *Elohim*'s Kingdom will be lost forever. The felicity of Atlantis will be shattered and all traces of its name will be blown in the winds!"

Heavy silence reigned in the Hall of Kings and the Lucoman only bowed their heads when the Priest-King, blessing them, withdrew.

Nabor stayed with Amatur and Tenupo, the aged priest who patiently answered the numerous questions put to him by the two young men.

"When I called you in my distress, dark beings were harassing me. Their cold breath touched me and I felt, as though grabbed by dark hands," Nabor told him.

Tenupo nodded, "Those were beings from the Realm of Shadows where the souls of the Dark Ones go when the days of their earthly existence come to an end. They don't have the pure consciousness that the children of Eya-Eya have, they don't know anything about *Elohim*, His laws and His Kingdom of Light. They are not familiar with the brilliance of the Eternal Light and do not long for it in their hearts. Nonetheless—the creative impulse is also alive in them and the time is near when they will be shown the path."

Amatur asked respectfully, "Will it be beneficial for Atlantis when the Dark Ones' minds become enlightened?"

"In so far as the sons of Eya-Eya keep their faith and continue treading *Elohim*'s paths, they will be the teachers and guides of the Dark Ones. But if they fall from their height, they will be like the others and unspeakable misery will come over Atlantis." And, bidding them farewell, he added, "If you give support to each other in your endeavor, you can't fail." Finally, turning to Nabor, he remarked in warning, "Don't, however, allow your zeal to make you forget that you are also the ruler of your country; it is your responsibility from now on to fulfill both these tasks!"

The night was mild, a gentle breeze was blowing, softly caressing those who lay asleep in their palaces and houses. After the heat of the day the nights were like an invigorating fountain of strength in the land of Eya-Eya. Lying on his couch, the Lucoman of Maya was breathing in the fragrant air. The curtains in his room had been pulled back; the sounds of the night were mingling with the regular roll of the waves on the shore below.

Nabor was dreaming. In his dream he saw the distant Beloved, the Beautiful One who had slipped from his hands, floating charmingly and enticingly through the images of his dream—for the loving yearning was still in him. "Maya," he whispered in his sleep. And again, while his arms stretched out longingly, "Maya!" Then, abruptly, he sat up in terror, looking around him. He was alone; his hands had reached out into the void and he had been awakened by his own movement. Alone and lonely! The realization of his condition rose inside him painfully. "Am I to go through life in solitude?" he asked himself. "I am still young and the thirst for life is burning in my blood still! I will set out and search for her—for the one who seems lost forever. But I'm going to find her wherever she might be. I'm going to find her by wandering along the path of my soul...."

Since that one time in the Temple of Bayagard, he had never again tried to leave his bodily sheath. To try again, he called *Elohim* for protection first, then he let himself glide into meditative absorption. Soon his body turned stiff, while his bodily awareness died away slowly and he gradually began swinging in holy silence. There was not a stir within him and the clarity of superconsciousness began rising within him. Light enveloped him, carried him ahead. In this flood of light he saw the hieroglyph MAYA. At that moment he freed himself from his sheath with a bolt and was immediately pulled up and away—as if seized by a cyclone. At once he found himself in the fore-court of a temple were he saw Maya in a white robe surrounded by a large crowd of people. She was dancing a sacrificial dance in front of a stone altar upon which a fire was burning. Nabor moved up to her closely and breathed her name into her ear. Maya's eyes widened in fright, her hands moved to push away the cause of her fear—then she collapsed with a scream. Those standing around her busied themselves with the unconscious priestess, carrying her into the temple.

After some moments Maya opened her eyes and her gaze passed over the young Tursian women who stood by her bed in sorrow. "Where is my child? Bring my son to me!"

A pretty little boy with blond hair and blue eyes was carried in by an elderly woman. She handed the child to Maya, who pressed the boy to her heart. "Guweil," she said tenderly—but the very moment her hands gently caressed his hair, she had the distinct feeling that she had been touched by a soft stirring of air. Her heart missed a beat—and she drew her child to her even more desperately. There!—she was quite certain, a hand as if made of light was reaching out for Guweil!

"No, no!" she cried out. "Guweil is mine! I will not give him up!"

The young priestesses of the Sun stepped away from her: their mistress had obviously lost her mind! They must inform Wea.

In the course of the following months the ruler of the Mayan Kingdom became feverishly active. He visited the blacksmiths' workshops daily, watching them manufacturing countless spear tips and daggers out of a coldly gleaming metal—a metal the Atlanteans had learned could be transformed into deadly weapons as soon as it came out of the fire, where it was tempered.

"What is the Lucoman up to?" the entire court wondered. Many different rumors began circulating in Mayagard.

Nabor had ships built, big ships—and he ordered thousands of young men to be trained in the handling of the new weapons, but nobody dared to ask him about his intentions. He remained aloof and his gaze remained distant as he moved through the unrest he was causing.

The palace officials, chamberlains and advisers tried to find out from Amatur the reason for these unusual preparations. The priest told them gravely, "All I can tell you is that the Lucoman is treading the road of self-generated destiny." All other questions he left unanswered. Amatur's heart was worried about his friend—and yet, he too did not ask him—only Tenupo's words came back to him: "…the time is near when the Dark Ones will be shown the path…."

The sanctuary of the Sun-God was set in a surrounding of mountains covered with dense forests. The Sun Temple itself—put together from tightly fitted square granite stones, stood on a high hill. A spacious fore-court fenced in by a wall, accommodated the sacrificial altar, in front of which had been placed a mighty hollowed-out stone resembling a large, tilted basin. Like all ceremonies of worship, this one also began when the first rays of the rising sun were caught in the hollow space inside the tilted stone's cavity. Then priests and priestesses began circling the sacred stone and the altar upon which a fire had been lit. The High Priest Sandor seized the sacrificial animal at exactly that moment with a hard grasp: a flashing dagger—blood sprouting forth and the immolated animal expired on the altar's steps. Young priests lifted up the body of the animal and threw it on the altar fire.

Now long horns were being sounded, producing dull, deep sounds, and cymbals rang out rhythmically, as Maya—surrounded by both male and female temple dancers—appeared on the scene. Amidst the dark-haired Tursians, she looked like a being of light with her blond beauty. Gradually the dance offered to the Sun-God grew increasingly wild. On that day, Wea stood near the Temple's gates with his captains, observing Maya. She had not become his, as he had hoped. More unattainable than ever, she was living in the Temple's precincts as a priestess and her son with her.

The sun disk rose majestically—and was greeted with exultant chanting. Maya stopped in her dancing. With her arms held out toward the sun, she looked the enthralling image of a goddess. Finally the chanting dissolved the spell which seemed to have charmed her—and she swiftly disappeared into the Temple with the other dancers. Meanwhile, a troop of horsemen came up the hill toward the Temple on their small, shaggy horses. When they had reached the gates, the first one of these riders slid down from his sweat-covered mount and threw himself to the ground before Wea.

"What is it?" the Prince growled.

"There are a great number of ships landing on the shore and giants with light-colored skin as numerous as the trees of the forest are pouring out of them, assembling and headed in this direction through the forest," he stammered, the words tumbling out of his mouth.

"Why didn't you stop them by barring their way?" Wea asked, grinding his teeth in suppressed fury.

"How are we to bar the way to—gods?" the man replied horrified.

"You fools!" the Prince shouted. "They are human beings of flesh and blood like you and I and a fitting target for our spears!"

Wea did not lose much time, now. His short orders made his officers rush off in all directions. Loud trumpet sounds began to fill the air, propagating themselves throughout the Tursian Empire.

Maya was playing with her son, when a dark shadow suddenly filled the door. Frightened, the child sought shelter by pressing against his mother. Wea walked into the room, his features forbidding.

"The Atlanteans are approaching in great numbers," he said, his voice gloomy and heavy.

"It's Nabor! I knew he'd come; he wants the child!" Maya whispered, her voice expressionless. But she recovered immediately and—straightening up, her green opalescent eyes glittering dangerously—she exclaimed, "He is not going to get him!"

"That's right, my Queen," Wea agreed. "The trumpets are already being sounded to round up my warriors for the hard fighting ahead. It looks like this arrogant pack of 'shining gods' will bleed to death in my forests...."

There was great activity along the coast. The Tursians, shy and submissive, obeyed the orders given them by the Mayans and threw their weapons away willingly, piling up high heaps of spears and daggers. The Lucoman ordered some of the tribal chiefs to be brought to him. Offering them gold and precious stones against as many horses as they could bring him. Eseko served as interpreter making them understand his master's wishes. The Tursians stared greedily at the glittering rings and bracelets in the golden chests Nabor had placed before them. It did not take long for them to bring the desired horses—in fact, entire herds were driven out of the forests for him. The Mayas for their part had great fun with the small, shaggy animals. They put bridles on them and tried out many daring equestrian feats. Just as Nabor was choosing an especially strong animal for himself, Eseko came up to him, saying, "Sire, Wea's fortress is on a high rock many days from here; nearby, I am told, is the Sun Temple, where the 'goddess', as the Tursians call her, is said to dwell. But," he added, "the journey to that place is full of dangers: one would have to travel along a narrow trail across mountains covered with dense forests." Weighing this information, Nabor knew that should there be a battle, the Tursians would certainly attack from ambushes set up in the forests and that the realization of his goals would be reached only at a cost of many lives.

With these thoughts, he looked around at his men—these carefully selected sons of the Mayan Kingdom who at the height of their youthful strength and beauty had followed him in full confidence, unaware that they were headed for danger and death. The very thought made him shudder. Blood would flow—precious human blood, and that blood would come down on him! Did he really have the right to sacrifice other fathers' sons in order to win back his own child?

Premenio approached with some of the palace officials, and as Nabor looked up at him, he asked, "Sire, the men are waiting for your signal. Are we to sound the bugles and break camp?"

"Put up sentinels on all sides of the camp! Have the forest patrolled by scouting squads to check out any possible danger that might threaten us."

Everybody looked at him in surprise, only the aged Eseko nodded in understanding.

"It is your intention, then, to stay in this place, Sire?" Premenio asked sullenly.

"The men are to camp here until I call them for action," was the Lucoman's chilly answer, as he motioned the delegation to leave. Soon cheerful camp life set in. At nightfall fires were lit in a circle, Atlantean songs and hymns rang out. The sound of the singing reached Nabor's tent. He was alone. The battle of thoughts was still raging within him. So far he had been struggling to come to a clear decision in vain. He sank back into the soft cushions of his divan, exhausted, and began praying to *Elohim* for help in taking the right road. He waited quietly, listening within all the while. A long time passed before the subtle inner voice could be heard whispering, "Wrestle with Wea's soul! If you don't succeed in subduing it, return home!"

The Tursian warriors prepared for war. Everywhere in the country the tribal elders and chiefs gathered their men and led them toward the coast. Wea held a war council: "First we'll let them penetrate our forests as deeply as possible—then we'll wear them down. Every day and each night we'll terrify them; our spears will simply not stop whirring and whistling around their heads.

The proud Lucoman's blond giants will fall and their blood will soak our earth. Dead or alive, bring me Nabor!"

The following day the message arrived that the Atlanteans were camping along the beach. The Tursian prince laughed out contemptuously. "He is avoiding battle! His men are just as yellow-bellied as he is! We'll chase them around a little and then, drive them into the sea" he said, adding the order, "Keep your men ready! When the night recedes and dawn breaks, I'll take them into battle."

After this announcement Wea felt as if driven to see Maya. He said to her, "Your husband, my Queen, is lingering on the coast. His funky heart is reticent to start the fight." Maya was intrigued by what she was hearing, but she remained silent when he continued triumphantly,

"This is why he will be smashed by Tursian power—or simply be pushed back into the sea."

Maya's Atlantean origins began stirring within her. Since the visionary moments at the Sun Temple, she had been unable to free herself from troubled foreboding. What good would the battle-tried Tursian armies be against the powers of the occult arts?

"Be careful, Wea," she said warningly. "Nabor is more dangerous than you think!"

Wea only answered with an arrogant shrug of his shoulders. However, after a short silence he said demandingly, "If the courage of my men destroys the invaders—thus deflecting the danger from both you, my Queen, and your blond offspring, and when—crowned with glory—they return home to the waiting arms of their loving wives, I also hope to find the wife in you—not the priestess or only the Queen!"

"If you open the road for me, you will be granted that fulfillment," Maya whispered, turning away from him.

"I'll take you at your word, my Queen!"

"I'll crush that coward under my heel and Maya will be mine," Wea, full of self-assurance, said to himself. He sat with his captains, drinking deep into the night. It was a noisy togetherness with much loud laughter until they left the great hall of his fortress in the early hours. Wea went to bed—and soon his deep breathing indicated that he had fallen asleep. Heavy darkness reigned in his bed-chamber. Suddenly, the prince started groaning in his slumber, turning this way and that. Then silence reigned again. But soon, once more, a muffled groan was heard. Eventually Wea became increasingly agitated as if he had fallen victim to a nightmare. After much groaning he suddenly uttered a wild cry and sat up in his bed. Realizing that his room was filled with a bluish-purple light which seemed to be getting lighter and lighter, he wondered whether he was dreaming or awake. He rubbed his eyes—and knew: this is no dream! The entire hall was lit up by this light so brightly he was able to distinguish every object it contained. There—a figure was forming in the light! Wea stared at the apparition with unbelieving eyes and realized that it was approaching slowly, as if hovering. Then he recognized the face! It was the face of the one he hated so much. The eyes in the detested face were enormous and pinning him down with a commanding stare. The Prince was seized by cold terror, paralyzing him to the point of physical pain. He closed his eyes—but upon opening them again, he saw that the apparition was still there. It had not gone away and those burning eyes continued to hold him relentlessly. Indeed, the face came closer and closer! Wea sprang out of bed and fled toward the wall with an inarticulate cry—but the figure approached closer still. The Tursian managed to get to his feet firmly and started running across the hall but when he was about to move through the doorway, the figure was hovering there in front of him. He staggered back. Virtually out of his mind with fright and terror, the Prince snatched a dagger off the wall and began stabbing at the vision—but the blade only hit emptiness. Now Wea started rushing about the hall like a startled deer, hitting a massive wooden table here, a trunk there. He stumbled—fell and remained lying on the ground hiding his face in his trembling hands. Suddenly a voice breathed his name: "Wea!" He leaped to his feet again—and rushed out of the room. This time he succeeded in getting outside. Pale moonlight was all around. Screaming, he crossed the fore-court. Life began to stir in the other buildings as half-naked figures appeared. They saw their lord running around screaming at the top of his voice, his features twisted, his hair disheveled. A few courageous men went after him and when they were close enough, started to call his name, but Wea didn't hear them. He ran and ran, breathing with difficulty, panting. He headed toward the forest and, when he had reached it, went into the dense shrubs, disappearing in the enveloping thicket.

The next day he was found by a search party: he lay as if united with the earth in a cramp, with his face to the ground. When the men—who thought him to be dead—turned him over, it seemed to them as if his face was showing signs of life. And indeed—his eyes half opened as his lips mumbled incomprehensible sounds. One of the men brought his ear close to Wea's mouth and was able to hear the words: "The god of the Atlanteans beat me. Nabor is your master now!" The officer got up horrified and told his companions what he had heard. The news spread like wildfire amongst the Tursian soldiers, paralyzing their mettle. The officers decided to send a few chiefs to Nabor to declare their submission.

At the request of the captains, Maya was informed of the new situation by the High Priest Sandor.

"Nabor just hunted him down and finished him off," she thought. To her surprise, she felt relief at this realization.

After some days the scouts reported that the Atlanteans were approaching—and shortly afterwards Premenio appeared within the precincts of the Sun Temple with some of the cavalry. He transmitted Nabor's greeting to Maya, announcing the Lucoman's arrival on the next day.

Maya sat in her apartment, clad in the azure-blue royal coat with the boy on her lap. Lea, Wea's sister, a girl of great loveliness with black hair, dark eyes and tawny skin, was with her. The girl was engulfed in the depth of the grief Wea's disappearance had caused her as tears streamed down her face incessantly. Nobody knew where he had gone. Maya tried to console her with kindly words. "You'll stay with me, Lea, even if I have to return to Eya-Eya."

Suddenly the sound of horses' hooves was heard. Then shouting, and the noise of many voices reached the room. "He has come to take my child!"—a bitter line showed around Maya's mouth.

The Lucoman greeted the High Priest with a few friendly words which were translated by Eseko. Sandor accompanied them into the Temple, but stopped in front of Maya's apartment; Nabor entered alone. He bowed before his wife without a word. Incapable of any other motion, Maya had simply risen to her feet. Guweil stood beside her with his eyes wide with astonishment as he studied the magnificent garments worn by the tall blond man. A soft smile on Nabor's part—which the child reciprocated—made the boy lose his shyness and he went up to the Lucoman with uncertain, toddling steps. Delighted, Nabor seized the child up into his arms. "Guweil!" he said. The boy pressed his head to his father's cheek. A feeling of intense happiness went through the man, who clasped the child to him even harder, while Maya could only look at the floor. She had lost her game. Now Nabor spoke: "The mother of my son is free to come to Mayagard if she wishes to go with us."

Maya turned pale. Nabor's words were her sentence: not as Lucoman, not as his wife, did he intend to take her home—only as the mother of his—her!—child!

"I was consecrated as priestess of the Sun God. No other man's hand ever touched me," she said quickly.

"Am I to understand that you wish to stay in this place?" Nabor asked, betraying no emotion at all.

"If I wanted to stay on, you would simply take my child away from me—and that I could not bear," came Maya's agonized answer.

"Guweil does not belong to you—nor to me! His call is to become—one day—the ruler of the Mayan Kingdom. He will be trained for that office, that's my duty. It is with a view to that obligation that I have come to this country; I am here to fetch him, to return his rights to him—rights that you deprived him of." Then, in a more conciliatory tone, he added, "If you want to remain the boy's mother, you are welcome. You will be allowed to spend time with him every day, but he will never be with you unattended."

"Which means that I will be held like a prisoner!" Maya burst out defiantly.

"Your obstinate mind has hardly changed! You broke your word as Lucoman and you broke your word with regard to your husband—the word you solemnly gave in *Elohim*'s Temple. You have forfeited the right to be trusted!"

Proud Maya's head bent down as if under blows.

Finally Nabor said, "You have until tomorrow morning to decide whether your heart tells you to be a mother or a priestess. Meanwhile I'm going to wait for your answer in Wea's Fortress. The mother of my son will be led back in all honors; the priestess of the Sun.... I will simply not notice." He turned away abruptly and left the room with the boy in his arms.

Maya cried out loud, "My child!" before breaking down overpowered with pain. Lea—forgetting her own sorrow—caressed her consolingly.

Nabor appointed Premenio to be Governor. Premenio was assisted in his new office by old Eseko, whose linguistic skills were needed. The larger part of the Mayan army was to stay with them in Tursia. Nabor took with him as hostages a number of Wea's captains and a few hundred of ordinary men. Maya, too, was on board one of the ships returning to Atlantis. Mamya, her Steward, had been ordered to stay with her, but she paid no attention to her former confidant. She only tolerated Lea's presence. When Nabor stepped on board the leading vessel, all sails went up and—swelling out in the wind—propelled the ships out to sea.

Nabor made his way through Mayagard in an unequaled and unprecedented triumphant procession. In his arms he held his son Guweil who pressed anxiously against his father. An overwhelming wave of cheer rose up toward the ruler, who gave instructions to lead the procession toward the Temple. Thereafter having been welcomed by the deeply moved Amatur—he gave thanks to *Elohim* for the Grace He had so palpably granted him. Then the Lucoman handed his son over to the young priest, saying, "May he grow up in *Elohim*'s Hall under your protection and guidance so that he can develop a believing heart and become a willing instrument of the Almighty!"

"He is a royal child, don't forget, Nabor!" Amatur replied.

"His young mind has been exposed—however briefly!—to a foreign people's mistaken faith. *Elohim* and the *Light* are still unknown to him. Plant the seed of true religion and love in his heart! Nobody could do that better than you, Amatur, my heart's only friend," Nabor said emphatically and added, "If Guweil calls for his mother, have her fetched for him, but never let her be alone with him!"

Lonely and shunned by all, Maya lived in the large house which had once served as guest house for Wea. By order of the Lucoman, the house had been refurbished in exquisite elegance. In all other respects, everything Maya might be in need of was placed at her disposal. She was, however, barred from access to the Lucoman's Palace and the Palace of the Thousand Columns. She realized with painful clarity that she had become a stranger in this country—and that she was also considered one by the people *and treated as such*. The invisible wall she once imagined and wanted so much to break down had become a reality. Her only confidante was Lea. The Tursian girl maintained the connection with the Tursian prisoners who had been housed outside of Mayagard. Motherly longing often drove Maya to see her child. Amatur always welcomed her with unchanged friendliness and brought the boy to her at once. As time went by, however, Maya noticed a change in the child's behavior. While he had run up to her happily at the beginning, he now hesitated before letting go of Amatur's hand. For Maya this discovery was the most bitter thing of all and she began to keep to her apartment for several days at a time, did not answer Lea's worried questions and hardly touched the food the Tursian girl brought her. Soon Lea was at her wit's end and had to call Mamya. In her poor Atlantean she explained to him that Milady was ill and that her mind was becoming deranged. "I'm going to have a look at her," the Steward said.

Accompanied by Lea, he went to Maya's apartment immediately. Surprised when she saw him, she asked what he wanted.

"Forgive me, Milady, but," he answered, motioning to Lea, "I heard you were ill and needed help."

"Ill? No—I'm not ill, Mamya. Perhaps my heart is slowly turning to stone but in order to prevent this from happening, I want to serve as Priestess of the Sun for the benefit of the foreign prisoners. Inform the Lucoman of my decision. There is nothing here to keep me—even my child has been alienated from me. I am going to leave this house this very day—this house in which I am a stranger. I am going to the Tursians to share their predicament!"

The Steward left without comment. The former Lucoman's power and magnificence were lost—indeed, the last trace of the proud Queen was about to vanish; he knew that nobody would even care to look her way when she left them....

Nabor listened to Mamya's report stoically. "Give her everything she asks for and let her go in peace," was his answer. His mind was preoccupied with other things just then—things that seemed more important than the fate of a woman who had left him and from whom he had struggled free. His plan to bring Atlantean culture to the Tursian people had been expanding rapidly of late. Almost daily, ships left from Mayagard with farmers and craftsmen on board who were to become the teachers of the Tursians on the other side of the ocean. Messengers travelled to and fro on smaller seaworthy vessels. They informed the Governor of the Lucoman's wishes and brought back Premenio's reports and suggestions.

Nabor had given strict orders not to touch the Tursian cult of the Sun-God. He recommended to Premenio that he become friendly with the High Priest Sandor and maintain that friendship. "Let them keep the faith of their ancestors—but win their hearts to make their souls open up. Maintain good discipline among your men in order for them to be a guiding example to those they are called upon to lead onward. Don't tolerate any opposition on the part of the Tursians, but spare their lives! I have put a heavy burden upon your shoulders, but the power you wield is great, too. Use that power carefully! Always consider that only a mild hand can pacify and unite opposites. Erect a temple on top of a high rock on the coast where praise and thanks will be given to *Elohim*, our God!"

Other messages were sent to his father and to Cerbio. The old Lucoman sent back word that he wished Nabor to come to see him together with Guweil, as Lehuana, Nabor's mother, was too old now and too weak to undertake the long journey to Mayagard to embrace her son and grandson.

"Mother!" thought Nabor. "I almost forgot about her in the confusion of my entanglements." And he gave order to prepare for his immediate departure.

He persuaded Amatur to come along as Guweil's personal attendant. They spent many joyful and happy hours within Bayagard's walls. Lehuana and Ebor surrounded their son with loving care, and little Guweil quickly conquered his grandparents' and his uncle Sebor's hearts. Everybody spoiled the lively child.

Nabor came back to life. All the hardship and worries which had caused his face to become so thin and serious dropped away from him. He spent much time with his mother; they would sit hand in hand on her couch and no spoken word disturbed their harmonious togetherness. Lehuana's misgivings had all come true and her heart had suffered with her son. She had made countless fervent prayers on his behalf to the God of Light and Love—prayers that had been heard! *Elohim* had safeguarded her child and given her a grandson who made her old heart gush forth with boundless tenderness. To everybody's delight Cerbio had also arrived, joining them with his mother Hethara. The two queens were old friends. Hethara had aged; her hair had turned as white as snow in the wake of the secret grief that was eating away at her heart—the sorrow surrounding her husband, whom she knew to be exposed to the desolate conditions of the North and from whom she had never heard again.

Cerbio was bubbling over with vivacity. His easy-going nature charmed Nabor. The young Wayan Lucoman was enthusiastic about his friend's plans and asked to be allowed to visit the land of the Tursians. Nabor granted the request immediately, seeing Cerbio's unrestrained and positive response to his projects. He sat down with the friend and they worked out more and more possibilities, one more audacious and enthralling than the next.

"The sons of Atlantis must become masters of the sea. They must become the guides of the Dark Ones in the Dark Ones' own country and lead them to a better life and more enlightened knowledge." Nabor's words were spoken with great adoration and Cerbio's reply was nothing short of awe: "You have been chosen from amongst all the kings! Speak to them in Bayagard! They will listen to you and they will follow you."

As a consequence, the three Lucoman set out together for Bayagard and Amatur came along with them. Guweil was left in his grandmother's care; Hethara also stayed on as Lehuana's guest.

The Great Hall of the Lucoman's Palace at Bayagard was filled with much cheer. Nabor's victory had caused general jubilation.

In the young Lucoman, it had kindled a desire to accomplish feats as great as he had, whereas the older rulers were glad that the danger had been stalled. On the other hand, they shook their heads when Nabor submitted his far-reaching plans to the Council. A lively discussion ensued, where all the pros and cons were debated. The young members argued against the older ones and vice versa. Nabor tried, with as much eloquence as he could find, to refute all objections—but to no avail. The golden and silver balls used for the ballot were equal in number. According to Atlantean law, the Loki must be called in to decide in such cases where a clear majority had not been reached.

Nabor was disappointed but Cerbio encouraged him, "Cheer up! The Loki cannot disregard our good reasons and we, the young generation, are all on your side." Uttering these words, the expression on his face was so solemn that Nabor involuntarily burst out laughing.

Later on, in the Hall of Kings, when the Loki had arrived amidst the Lucoman and had, as customary, blessed each one of them individually, he turned to the ruler of the Mayan Kingdom, saying,

"Tell me about your plans, Nabor!"

Hesitatingly at first but soon with increasing liveliness Nabor reported on the journey to Tursia. He described the Tursians' hard life, their religious practices, their customs and morals which left no room for the respect of human life.

The Loki listened quietly.

Encouraged by this reaction, Nabor continued with emphasis, "Isn't it the duty of the sons of Eya-Eya to let the Dark Ones participate in their way of life? To ease their path and to do all we can to lead them toward *Elohim* and his Realm of Light?"

The Priest-King's eyes turned away from Nabor, his gaze drifting off into the distance. His eyelids closed.

An intense silence reigned in the room. Minutes passed and still Huatami had said nothing. When his eyes finally opened, he said, "Your good intentions do your honor, Nabor, but you must know that the time has not yet come for the children of Atlantis to reach out their brotherly hands to the Dark Ones. The consciousness of these people is too narrow as yet, their souls too immature for them to understand our nature."

"When they are shown the goal and the path, they will follow," Nabor objected.

"Your efforts will be wasted! They have no desire to reach the Light, their senses arc enthralled by the illusory appearances of existence. Believe me, my son, I could reveal to you the true reason for the existence of these discrepancies between human civilizations but my lips are sealed by a holy vow. I cannot reveal the secret which was communicated by the light-filled God solely to the High Priest. Let our grand ancestors' terrible fate be a warning to you and all those who—blinded by your bloodless victory—hope for similar achievements for themselves. It was not for the conquest of an empire that you were protected by the Powers of Light and granted the gushing fountain of inner strength; it was to make good the injustice done to the young dauphin and to bring him back to the house of his forebears. It was these facts that activated the motivating impulse behind *Elohim*'s display of power in this case—and also behind your own heart's intent! Be content, Lucoman, with what you were able to achieve and give thanks to God for having returned your son to you, unharmed. Call your men back from the foreign land, for they will never be able to pull the Dark Ones up to their own level of understanding. You are only exposing your men to unnecessary danger—and with them, Eya-Eya's happiness."

Nabor turned pale; was he to destroy his own achievement?

"It cannot be *Elohim*'s will for human beings, our brothers, to live like wild beasts," he remonstrated. "The Light God's Love encompasses all creatures. We have no right to act otherwise. It is true that I wanted to retrieve my son. Obtaining him had been the initial motive for the journey to that country where I found disease, poverty and death torturing ignorant human beings. We cannot leave them to the mercy of the Dark Powers in whose fetters they are caught, passing their days in fear. My deed, which had been started with intentions coming from a pure heart, must now be carried through to perfection and I am going to commit myself to that task to my last breath."

"So—you refuse to obey *Elohim*'s Law?"

"It isn't *Elohim*'s Law! If it were *Elohim*'s wish to leave human beings to succumb to their misery, He would not be the God of Love!"

"Silence, insolent one! You are desecrating this place by your blasphemous words," Huatami shouted at him. "If you break the Law, misery will befall *you*—just as it befell your arrogant wife!"

"My wife," Nabor met the challenge as soon as he had regained some control over his anger, "my wife erred due to a dark impulse, but I, too, erred up to this hour, for I saw in you the intercessor between *Elohim* and us."

The Priest-King came up toward Nabor menacingly, his eyes aglow with a hard glint.

"Your crazy fancy will destroy Eya-Eya's peace. You are about to plant a terrible seed by turning your back on *Elohim* and disregard His Law. *May you be cursed*, you mischief-maker! You are preparing the ruin of Atlantis!"

Deadly pale, Nabor moved back one step, but having recovered his composure, he walked toward the door, where Cerbio and other young men surrounded him.

"You stay where you are—but I must follow the path my heart is dictating within me!" he told them.

"We stand by you, for we think like you," Cerbio replied for them all. At this, Ebor also left his column and, bowing down before the Loki, declared, "My son's path is also my path!"

All the while Huatami had been standing there as motionless as a stone. His ascetic features trembled—and then his lips whispered,

"Help me, *Elohim*! Give me a sign, so that they, too, can see your might and become aware of the positive motivation behind my zeal!" No sign appeared, but suddenly Huatami's eyes opened wide as if he were seeing a gruesome vision. His face became contorted as if in great pain and a loud groan escaped his mouth, as he exhaled with increasing difficulty. With trembling lips he uttered the following words which fell into the silence of the

Hall like heavy drops, "The greed for power is taking hold of them; they are conquering the Earth.... There is blood—much blood—they're turning their backs...they're turning their backs on *Elohim*!" His final, pain-wracked words were filled with lament. Then, once more, the old priest started groaning as he continued, saying, "The disaster will come—the great flood—many thousands of people scream and beg for their lives, but the flood engulfs them...." The Priest-King stumbled forward—and collapsed like a tree that had been felled. His head hit the marble floor. The Lucoman still present in the Hall of Kings stood paralyzed by the horror of what they saw. Lying on the floor, the Loki stammered, "Mercy—mercy—*Elohim*!—mercy!" And rising up once more with his last strength, he shouted the words so loud they echoed through the building like thunder, "Mercy, *Elohim*—mercy!" Then he fell back. A last convulsion went through his body, his eyes turned glassy, his mouth twisted in pain—and froze: Huatami had been called back. The Lucoman stood there, stunned.

Priests came to take care of the body and carried it out of the Hall, the place, where through spite and passion Eya-Eya's happiness had been destroyed.

The high-ceilinged room was quiet. An iridescent glow was reflected from the walls—a mysterious luminosity which lit up the couch on which Erik von Lichtenau lay asleep. His breathing was scarcely perceptible. From time to time a slight quiver crossed his features before his breathing became deeper and more regular. His body stretched, a deep sigh expanded his chest. As if searching for something, his hand glided along the edge of the couch—then he slowly lifted his eyelids. How heavy they were! Tired, he closed them again. Thousands of images were now rushing through his mind, which was, however, unable to form one single thought. Faces flashed up—one here, another there—but where had he seen them? Oh, yes, in his dream—a dream of inexpressible beauty...except the end, of course. The end had been bitter.

Eventually, re-opening his eyes and allowing his gaze to travel around the magnificent apartment in this grotto, it all felt like a gentle smile inside of him. He stretched his limbs comfortably and, again, his mind slipped off into a state of waking reverie. More images rose up before his mental eye. He saw himself ride along in a chariot drawn by a team of four spirited horses. He saw a large crowd of people in multicolored garments waving at him, calling his name, again and again: Nabor! Nabor! He saw himself waving back at them—and he saw a large ruby set in a broad golden ring sparkling on his finger. Involuntarily he moved his hand again to repeat the sparkling of the ring—when he suddenly awakened fully: There on his hand, still up in the air as if caught halfway through the waving motion—he saw the large ruby he had worn in his dream. Awake now, he touched the stone with his left hand in disbelief. It was the royal ring of Atlantis! "It's the ring which was given me by the old priest" he whispered, thoughtfully. But who were those people cheering at him and calling *"Nabor! Nabor?"* Wasn't that the name the old priest had called him? Again he closed his eyes—aghast. And again images began their multicolored play before him. Veil after veil fell away. Looking back thus into the past, he relived Nabor's—his!—life in short sequences of images. I was Nabor! The very thought of it held him transfixed.

But how could that be? On the other hand...this room...this ring...the old sage.... It must be the truth, no doubt about it. This adventure, which felt so real seemed also like a wonderful dream, like something that was now being integrated into his consciousness. Suddenly he knew: "I was repudiated because—although in good faith—I erred and I did not find my way back into the Realm of Light. For thousands of years I had to wander through many lives until I finally attained this knowledge. And Huatami...?" Then suddenly he had a flash: Huatami—that was the old sage! Hadn't Lehuana, his mother, said so too?—But where was Huatami now?

Lichtenau rose to his feet, left the room and stepped out into the corridor leading forth into the labyrinth. He began running—

until he came to the grotto with the stone figures of the royal couples, who seemed to smile at him. But he was driven forward; suddenly he knew with the certainty of a sleep-walker what he must do. Soon he noticed a flickering light in the distance. He went toward it—and wound up standing in front of the field of ruins and debris stretching out into the sunlight before him. A loud cry of relief rose up from within. Still blinded by the unaccustomed daylight, Lichtenau looked down—and saw Paolo who, by then, had also recognized him and was jumping about with joy. "Señor," he shouted, "Señor, you are alive! The Holy Virgin has heard my prayers!" And he made the sign of the cross. Coming up the slope running, he would not stop until he stood, panting, before the young scientist. Staring at him as if he were a ghost, he walked around him in circles.

"Truly, Señor, is it you?" And having calmed down a little, he went on, "Where was the Señor for so long? I've been looking for you everywhere in that damned grotto, but couldn't find a trace."

"I was in a world long since sunken into oblivion, Paolo," Lichtenau replied. Then he asked, "How long was I gone?"

"The sun set seven times, Señor."

Lichtenau sat down on the ledge of a rock and, pulling Paolo down to his side, he said, "Poor friend, you really had to wait a long time!"

"I didn't stay here all the time, Señor. After I had searched for you in vain, I rode back to the hotel and went through your things. I found a card with a Mexican name: Juanita y Serestro, in Mexico City. I sent a cable to her and received this answer," he said handing Lichtenau a telegram.

Lichtenau had listened in surprise and took the telegram. He read, "expect us—stop—are coming to Merida—stop—Juanita y Serestro." Juanita? Ah, Juanita, the dear girl!

"I'll never forget what you've done for me, Paolo," Lichtenau said deeply moved, squeezing the Mestizo's hand. Then he gave a start.

"Where did I see that face before," he thought. "The fire in those dark eyes? Wea!" The realization struck him like lightening. "Wea is Paolo—the same person!" Wea—in that past life—had taken his wife away from him! "There is a lot he's got to make up for to you"—the old sage had said. And hadn't some foreigner taken Paolo's fiancée away from him in this life? Did wrongdoing have its effects on oneself thousands of years later? "God's mills grind slowly," the old saying echoed through his mind. Paolo observed him, puzzled. What was the matter with the Señor?

Lichtenau composed himself, eagerly thinking that he must find the old sage again....

"We must return to the grotto, Paolo!" he said, rising to his feet. "Señor! In the name of the Holy Virgin—don't do that. You've been returned to the living once, don't challenge your fate a second time!" the Mestizo implored him.

"Don't worry, Paolo, I know the way—and your eyes will see wonderful sights," Lichtenau reassured him.

Lichtenau went in first, Paolo followed hesitatingly. The young German traced his steps back to the grotto with the statues and, turning off from there, followed the path the old sage had led him.

"Where is the large rock?" he wondered to himself, muttering. The light of his flashlight was moving across the wall while his fingers felt for the fine fissures in the stony surface. He was certain that it had been here that the old man had moved the rock and laid bare the entrance to the tunnel leading to the great chamber.

"Forget it, Señor! You'll never have enough strength to move these rocks aside," the Mestizo said with an ironic touch to his voice. Taken aback, Lichtenau stopped in his endeavors. Had he come to the wrong spot? He returned to the grotto with the statues. Here he had met Huatami. It was torture to think that he had lost the old man.

There—a movement of air passed by him, touching him like a gentle breeze, stirring him out of his gloomy brooding—and, suddenly, he had clarity: Huatami, who repudiated him, had taken him back to his Atlantean dimension of consciousness to expiate his guilt.

"Huatami! Huatami—thank you!" Lichtenau cried out loud—and the multiple echo of his words came back softly: "...thank you!"

An elegant automobile stopped in front of a large office building on a busy boulevard in Mexico City. A young lady stepped hastily out of the limousine and disappeared through the revolving door.

"Is Señor y Serestro in his office?" she asked the boy working the elevator on her way up. Having received an affirmative answer, she hastened by the clerks and entered her father's office unannounced.

Señor y Serestro looked up—but before he could say a thing, he was embraced passionately and given a smacking kiss on the cheek.

"We must go on a trip right away, papa! He's met with an accident; we've got to help him! We've got to leave for Merida this very day!" Juanita sputtered forth excitedly.

"Who is 'he'?" Señor y Serestro asked, somewhat puzzled.

"Herr von Lichtenau!—Oh, papa! Don't you remember—the young scientist I told you about?" Juanita replied reproachfully.

"That won't be possible, child. I've go to attend several meetings over the next few days." Señor y Serestro shook his head doubtfully. Juanita was near tears—the tremble around the corners of her mouth was a telling sign! "But we can't just let him perish!" she cried out imploringly.

"The girl is in love," flashed through Señor y Serestro's mind.

He said, "All right then, my little princess, we'll go!"

Passionate caresses from his daughter were his reward—then the "little princess" disappeared as suddenly as she had come, to start preparations for the journey.

Lichtenau met father and daughter in Merida.

"I've told papa everything, Herr von Lichtenau, and when Paolo's telegram informed us that you were missing, papa immediately agreed to come here with me," Juanita said. Her eyes were shining with happiness and pleasure to find her secret love well and in good health.

Papa cleared his throat; he did not recognize his daughter, who was clearly head over heels in love with the blond young man.

"I am certainly delighted to see you have come back from the underworld safe and sound and I should be happy to have you as our guest in my house in Mexico City, if your plans allow it."

Lichtenau looked at Juanita whose eyes held the same plea.

"I'd be happy to, Señor y Serestro," he said quietly.

A young couple was resting on deck-chairs arranged for them on the sun-deck of the transatlantic liner.

"I'm looking forward to seeing your homeland very much," said the young, beautiful woman whose happiness shone brightly on her face. "Are you also happy about it, Erik?" she added, turning to the tall young man who lay stretched out in the chair beside her.

"I am very happy about it, Maya!"

Juanita looked up at him startled, why did he call her Maya? Then her clear laughter rang out cheerfully: "He's dreaming again, my stern husband!"

They sank their gaze into each other's. Two hands met in a tender clasp....